W9-AYE-893

South Beach
Sizzle

South Beach Sizzle

**SUZANNE WEYN AND
DIANA GONZALEZ**

Simon Pulse
New York London Toronto Sydney

If you purchased this book without a cover, you should be aware that this book is stolen property. It was reported as "unsold and destroyed" to the publisher, and neither the author nor the publisher has received any payment for this "stripped book."

This book is a work of fiction. Any references to historical events, real people, or real locales are used fictitiously. Other names, characters, places, and incidents are the product of the author's imagination, and any resemblance to actual events or locales or persons, living or dead, is entirely coincidental.

⋙ SIMON PULSE
An imprint of Simon & Schuster
Children's Publishing Division
1230 Avenue of the Americas, New York, NY 10020
Copyright © 2005 Suzanne Weyn

All rights reserved, including the right of reproduction in whole or in part in any form.

SIMON PULSE and colophon are registered trademarks of Simon & Schuster, Inc.

Designed by Ann Zeak
The text of this book was set in Garamond 3.

Manufactured in the United States of America
First Simon Pulse edition February 2005

10 9 8 7 6 5 4 3 2 1
Library of Congress Control Number 2004110709
ISBN 1-4169-0011-X

For Dineen Garcia,
who first generously showed us Miami,
and in doing so made this story possible.
With love,
Suzanne and Diana

One

"Ew! This is disgusting!" Lula Cruz shouted over the deafening sound of the wind. She pulled off her black, rectangular-framed glasses and wiped away tiny squashed bugs with the end of her white shirt. She'd been pelted with the little insect pests ever since they'd driven out onto the open expanse of the 17.6-mile Chesapeake Bay Bridge-Tunnel. "Put the top up! Please!" she requested.

The driver of the classic, silver BMW convertible—a slim, handsome guy with lively brown eyes and short, dark, blue-tipped hair—smiled, but shook his head. "I don't know how."

"Then raise the windows, at least," she suggested. "You have to do it. My window button doesn't work. I think you have the child lock on or something."

"Okay." He pounded on the electronic buttons at his side.

Bzzt. The window to her right went up. And then down again.

Bzzt. The window on her left went up . . .

. . . then down . . . then up.

"Jeff, what are you doing?" she asked.

"I can't drive and adjust the windows at the same time," he explained, speaking loudly over the sea breezes blasting them from the Atlantic Ocean. "I can't multi-task. I'm an evolutionary throwback to a simpler time."

Lula laughed and shook her head. "Maybe you're just a lunatic," she teased.

Jeff lurched into the next lane, causing Lula to grab the side of her seat. She decided to say no more and let him pay attention to driving. Since they'd left New York City at dawn that morning, Lula had come to a startling—and somewhat horrible—realization.

Jeff was a horrendous driver.

Totally berserk! He was the Ozzy Osbourne of automobiles.

She'd thought—just assumed—that she already knew everything about Jeff. But she hadn't known *this*.

Watching him grin with pleasure as he clutched the steering wheel made her smile. This was so typical of him. Naturally he would take a job driving a sporty, classic car to Florida even though he clearly had absolutely no idea what he was doing.

He'd found the help-wanted ad in *The Village Voice*. A man in New York had sold a BMW convertible on eBay to a woman in Florida. He needed a driver to deliver the car to her. He'd pay for gas and for Jeff's meals and would also pay him three hundred dollars for his so-called driving.

Jeff always got them mixed up in things like this. She remembered, for example, the time he'd volunteered them to run the frog-hop races at their community center's Kids' Day and they'd spent hours running after fugitive frogs.

But that was okay with her, really.

Jeff's offbeat, but always upbeat, optimism was one of the best things about him. He believed—no matter how disastrous things appeared at the moment—that everything would work out fine in the end. And, when they were together, Lula felt the same way.

So what if he was a complete freak of a menace on the road? She figured that you had to take the good with the bad when it came to people.

The good with the bad . . .

Lula slipped a pen and a small silver notebook from the large brown canvas bag she'd stowed under the front seat. *The good with the bad,* she wrote. She liked the way the phrase sounded and wanted to remember it for her next poem. It might even make a good title.

Looking up, she saw a red sports car dart dangerously close in front of them. Way too close! "Look out!" she cried.

Jeff swerved into the other lane. A terrible, crunching, grinding sound screamed up from the engine.

"What *was* that?" Lula shouted, alarmed.

"Not to worry," Jeff assured her. "I just threw it into the wrong gear." He shrugged and flashed a sheepish grin at her.

"Oh, is that all?" Lula said, leaning back into her seat. "Jeff, have you ever driven this kind of car before?"

"Do you mean a standard clutch?"

"Yeah."

"Once."

"Once?" she said warily.

"But it was for a whole hour," he added, as if that were equivalent to a PhD in driving a manual-shift car. "I may be a little inexperienced, but at least I know *how* to drive."

"Really?" she said, but he didn't seem to notice her sarcasm. Actually, she knew what he was getting at. Mass transportation was so easily available in the city that there was no real reason to learn to drive. That's why she had never gotten her license.

Reaching over her head, Lula gathered as much of her blowing hair as she could grab. With quick twists of her wrists, she bundled the thick, unruly strands into the black elastic she'd worn on her wrist. Stray pieces instantly escaped and danced around her forehead.

Jeff turned on the radio, and buzzing static blasted at them. They'd lost the signal of the rock station they'd been listening to in New York. Jeff fiddled with buttons until he found a station that came in clear, nearly crashing them into a passing car in the process.

Lula once again clutched the side of her seat and stared, wide-eyed, at Jeff. Just then, the station he had tuned in crackled to life and blasted "The Remedy," by Jason Mraz.

Jeff cranked the song to full volume.

Lula's mood lifted along with the music. It was the start of summer. They'd somehow managed to graduate—high school was behind them, finally! And they were together on this road trip to Florida. What could be better?

She put her glasses back on and knelt up on the seat, her arms stretched wide, and started singing along. Jeff sang, too, belting out the lyrics as he drove. "I won't worry my life away!"

That night Lula and Jeff sat on the hood of the car and finished their ice-cream cones. They'd stopped at a rest area off Interstate 95, at the edge of a city called Florence, in South Carolina.

Jeff suddenly grabbed her arm. "Okay, coming out the door right now," he said, dropping his voice. "Yours or mine?"

Trying not to be obvious, Lula skirted her eyes over toward the front door of the restaurant. A real hottie had just come out. Broad shoulders and cut abs were easy to see beneath his tight T-shirt. Form-fitting jeans promised a great walking-away view. "Mine," Lula said.

"Dream on," Jeff disagreed. "Look at those abs. That guy spends a *lot* of time at the gym."

"Check the hair, though," Lula countered. "No gay man would wear a mullet anymore."

Jeff shook his head. "I don't know. . . . I've seen some mullet-headed gay guys."

"Not in this lifetime," Lula argued.

A Dodge Ram pickup drove into the parking lot. Its driver was a cowboy type in a Stetson hat. He stopped, and the object of their attention climbed in. Jeff pounded Lula's shoulder excitedly. "Busted! I so win! Did you see that guy who just picked him up? I win!"

"You do not!" Lula disagreed. "That could have been his brother or his friend."

"Or his *boy*friend," Jeff added.

"Maybe," she allowed as her interest in the subject began to fade. "Who wants a guy who wears a mullet, anyway?"

"Well, this *is* the South," he allowed.

The South might as well have been a foreign country to her. New York, New York, was the only place she'd ever lived. "It's so far away from Manhattan, isn't it?" she said, already feeling a little homesick. "Where would we be right now if we were home?"

"Probably drinking too many caffe lattes at Rick's New Rican," he suggested. Rick's New Rican Coffeehouse was their favorite hangout.

On open-mike nights, Rick let Lula perform the poetry she wrote, even though she was younger than all the other poets. "Your stuff is good," he'd told her. "When you're good, age is just a number."

On her last night in the city, Rick had even given her a going-away pep talk. "Are you nervous about going to school in Miami?" he had asked.

"A little," Lula had admitted to him. "At first the University of Miami seemed too far away from home. But then I got the creative writing scholarship and it became so affordable, I couldn't really turn it down."

"They gave you a stash of cash, huh?"

"I don't know if I could go to college if they hadn't," she'd replied.

"Well, good luck, kiddo," Rick had said to her. "You might meet kids at this university who have fancier cars or nicer clothes, but remember: You have talent. You're a damn good poet. You have something in here"—he'd thumped his chest lightly—"that no one can ever take away from you. You have passion for life, and it shows in your writing."

"Thanks," she'd told him, wrapping him in a quick hug. In a few words, Rick had helped her deal with an anxiety that she hadn't even admitted to herself until that moment: How would she fit in at the University of Miami?

There on the Lower East Side of Manhattan she was in a crowd of other kids who were mostly like herself. They came from different ethnicities, but very few of them had a lot of money. If they did, they'd have been going to a private school. So, although she lived in a small apartment with her mother, living off the unreliable and usually insufficient money her mother made as an aspiring actress, Lula didn't think about her lack of money on most days. All the families around her struggled, and that's just how things were.

Now, though, she was going into a whole different world, where she wouldn't be with other people who were so much like herself. Would they look down on her because she might not have all things they did? She tried not to care. After all, it was a trivial, superficial thing. But sometimes she felt herself freeze up inside, overcome with anxiety.

Jeff's voice broke through Lula's thoughts, bringing her back. "Did your mom freak this morning when you left?"

Lula shook her head and scooped a drip of chocolate off the end of her cone with her tongue. "No, I think she was relieved that I'm not going to Canada with her." Lula's mom had just landed a big commercial acting job that was being shot in Canada. It was an important job for her since she hadn't worked in two months. "She knows I'd be bored up there, and she won't be around because she'll be busy shooting the commercial."

"She's making that foot-spray commercial, right?" Jeff said.

"Funk-Off foot spray," Lula confirmed.

Jeff snorted with laughter. "I love the name of that stuff."

Lula laughed too. "I know. She actually has to say, 'Spray foot fungus away with Funk-Off!'" That reminded Lula that she had brought a can of the stuff along to show Jeff. Wiping her chocolate-covered hands on the back of her jeans, she reached into her brown bag and pulled out the can. "Ta-da!"

"That's so sick!" Jeff cried. "I have to have this! Every time someone cuts me off on the road, I'm gonna shoot a blast of Funk-Off at them!"

Lula tilted her head back up at the dark

night sky and laughed. What a sight *that* would be.

Jeff hopped back into the car. "Come on. We have to go find a hotel. I can't drive anymore."

Lula sent up a silent cheer.

They drove a short way and came to a shabby but affordable-looking place called Fred's Hideaway. The heavyset man at the front desk asked them if they wanted one room or two. "One, I guess," Jeff said, glancing apprehensively at Lula to check if that was okay.

"Sure. One room," she agreed with a shrug. Neither of them had a lot of money. The less they needed to spend, the better.

The man leered at Lula with a knowing grin. She glared back at him. As he handed Jeff the room key, he winked. "Have fun," he said.

Jeff reached down to his overnight suitcase and pulled out the can of Funk-Off. He sprayed it around the room.

"Hey! What's that?" the man shouted.

"It's Funk-Off!" Jeff replied with a goofy, bright smile. "I thought you could use some."

"Get out of here with that stuff!" he yelled, turning three shades of red.

They hurried, snickering quietly, out of the office. "I can't believe you did that!" Lula managed to say when they were outside and able to burst into laughter.

"I had to do *something*," Jeff replied. "I hope the rest of this place isn't as dirty as his mind."

Their room was small and smelled of mildew, but it had two double beds. Lula threw herself down on the nearest one. "Wow, I'm beat. What time do you want to get up tomorrow?"

Jeff had already gone into the bathroom. He'd left the door open, and she could hear little blasts of an aerosol can being squirted. "What are you doing?" she asked.

"If there was ever a place that needed Funk-Off, this is it," he said as he squirted. "I think we've arrived at fungus headquarters."

She reached over to the small digital clock on the nightstand between the two beds. Arching a brow as she flicked off a questionable-looking bug, she called out to

Jeff, "What time do you want to get up tomorrow?"

"Five?" he suggested.

She groaned.

He stepped out of the bathroom, a toothbrush in his mouth. "I was hoping we could get to Florida tomorrow," he explained through a mouthful of tooth-paste.

"So soon?" she asked. She didn't want to spend an eternity driving with Jeff, the Menace of the Highway—that was for sure. But she hadn't expected to get to Miami the next day. She wasn't really ready for that yet.

A small, nervous knot clenched in Lula's stomach. Even though the University of Miami wouldn't begin until the end of summer, she'd convinced her mother to let her stay with her father, who lived in nearby Coconut Grove. That way she could learn her way around the Miami area before she started classes. And, with Jeff there, it was bound to be more fun than being alone in Alberta, Canada.

Her dad had been pretty much out of her life since her parents divorced when she was five. She'd e-mailed him and asked if she could stay with him. He didn't answer for two days, but when he did, his reply right was to the point: "Sure. The more the merrier! Come on down!"

Maybe this would be a good chance to get to know her father. On the other hand, it might be a complete disaster. She really didn't know what life with him would be like, and it made her nervous.

She'd find out . . . tomorrow.

TWO

"I can't get used to all these palm trees," Jeff remarked as they stopped at a traffic light. "Do you think they're real or made of plastic?"

"Plastic," Lula replied. "Definitely. I think we've driven into a postcard." This feeling of being in an unreal, unnaturally bright landscape had begun when they drove into Georgia and had intensified as they continued on down Florida's east coast.

Lula had the MapQuest directions to Jeff's uncle Frank's house pressed flat on her knee. Jeff was going to live with him while he searched for work in Miami. "Go left at the next light," she instructed him.

The left turn brought them into a neat neighborhood of ranch-style homes with perfectly groomed front lawns. Jeff stopped in front of number 94, his uncle's address. "This is it," he said, sounding decidedly nervous. "I don't really know my uncle Frank. He's an army guy, and he just retired this year."

Jeff had worked all through high school as a prep cook in restaurant kitchens, cutting, chopping, assembling, and garnishing foods for chefs. He liked the restaurant environment and wanted to learn more about it. He thought it might even be a career he'd like to pursue, but he didn't have the money to enroll in a culinary school.

A grill cook he worked with had told Jeff he might find it easier to find cooks and chefs who would teach him if he started outside Manhattan, where it wasn't as competitive. With that in mind, Jeff came to Miami hoping to be hired as kitchen help in a really top-notch restaurant and learn that way. His dream was to someday become a chef. He wasn't sure if

Miami was any less competitive than Manhattan, but it was the only city where he had a relative he could stay with.

"It was nice of your uncle to let you stay here," Lula said as they sat in the car in front of his uncle's house. "This way you can go find a job without paying for a motel."

"My mother is his big sister. I don't think he could say no to her," Jeff replied. He turned to Lula with pleading eyes. "Come in with me?"

"Okay," she agreed. Together they walked up the cement path and knocked on the door. Jeff rang the bell, and after a few moments a tall, neatly dressed man in his fifties appeared.

He stared at them with a wary expression. He seemed to have no idea who they were.

"I'm your nephew Jeff." Uncle Frank stared at them with a stony face. Jeff laughed nervously. "You know—Jeff Terrio. From New York. Your nephew, like I said."

His steely blue eyes were unwavering in his stone face. Lula was sure they must have the wrong address. "We're sorry," she said, starting to back up. "We were looking for Frank Malloy and——"

"You're at the right address, little lady," he interrupted. "I'm just surprised, is all."

"Surprised?" Jeff said. "I thought Mom told you that I——"

"I would never have expected my sister to allow her son to dye his hair blue."

"She likes it, actually," Jeff told him, a nervous quaver in his voice.

"And are you telling me she also likes it that you wear women's jewelry?" Uncle Frank went on, peering at the small silver hoop in Jeff's ear.

"Jeff's mom thinks guys with earrings are cool," Lula put in, feeling it was her duty as Jeff's friend to defend him. "I do too. A lot of the guys at our school have earrings. Some guys wear two, or even more."

Uncle Frank stared at her coldly. "Nor did I expect my nephew to arrive with a girlfriend in tow. There will be no sinful cohabitating in this house. You will have to find other accommodations, young lady. This is a decent household."

Jeff grabbed hold of Lula's arm and began backing up. "Not to worry, Uncle Frank," he said. "I'll be taking Lula to her dad's place. I just wanted to stop by and let you know I'd arrived. I'll drop her off and be back later."

"We lock our doors for the night at twenty-one hundred hours. Sharp!" he barked.

Lula and Jeff began counting frantically on their fingers. Jeff got there first. "Nine?" he said. "But it's already nearly eight now."

"Twenty-one hundred hours," he repeated, and shut the door.

"What a freak," Jeff said as they hurried back down the walkway toward the car.

A black-and-white pug dog came charging around the side of the house, yipping at them with a maniacal intensity. Lula and Jeff froze. "Do you think he heard what I said about his master?" Jeff whispered. He glowered at the dog. "I bet Uncle Frank has it trained to spy."

"I hope that's *all* it's trained to do," Lula muttered between lips clenched into a frozen smile. "Nice doggie," she attempted to soothe the barking dog. "Sweet poochie."

A deep, fierce growl rose up from the animal's thick throat. It bared its teeth and began to lunge toward them.

In a burst of speed, they ran for the car. The dog raced after them. Jeff dove headlong into the open convertible, Lula right behind him.

With a horrible grinding of gears, Jeff managed to start the car and speed away from the house. The barking dog chased the car for the entire length of the block before they lost sight of it.

"Well, that was enjoyable," Jeff said with a shudder as they turned out of the neighborhood and onto a main road.

Lula took out another set of MapQuest directions that would direct them to her father's address. In just minutes they were entering a community of condominium apartments. Several two-story buildings were clustered around a large man-made pond and connected by cement paths. "He's in building C," Lula said when they'd climbed out of the car.

He had lived here for the last twelve

and a half years, but she'd never seen it before. During those years she'd only seen him briefly, sometimes at weddings and mostly at family funerals. But she knew the building number from the return address of the birthday cards that came on most birthdays.

They found the building and the apartment. It was at the back of the complex and faced a long, rectangular community pool surrounded by a wooden fence.

Music blared from the apartment. Lula rang the buzzer, and they waited. No one came to the door. She looked into the window on her right. Through the partially open blinds she could see that there was a party going on inside. "Do you see your dad?" Jeff asked.

Lula nodded. It would have been difficult to miss him.

He was standing on a table singing along with a karaoke machine. Ruben Cruz was exactly as she remembered him: handsome, dressed in a half-buttoned Hawaiian shirt, and the life of the party.

Lula pressed the buzzer again and held it down. After a few more minutes, a blond woman opened the door. She was wearing a midriff top, tight short-shorts, and lots of makeup. She was probably in her late thirties. "Yes?"

"I'm Ruben's daughter," Lula said, suddenly feeling very shy.

The woman seemed confused. "Ruben has a daughter?"

"Yes!" Lula replied, with a note of exasperation in her voice.

About twenty other people were there. A few looked casually toward the door to see who had arrived. Others were too busy talking, dancing, eating, or drinking to notice them.

"Ruben!" the woman shouted over the noise and music. Ruben Cruz didn't hear her. His eyes were closed, and his arms were spread wide as he enunciated every syllable of "Baby Got Back."

"My homeboys tried to warn me, but that butt you got makes me so—" he raised a fist in the air to punctuate the next word but was cut off by the woman's shout.

"Ruben!"

He stopped and looked at her quizzically.

"There's a kid here who says she's your daughter!"

The music had stopped, and this time her words rang out loud and clear across the room. Everyone turned to stare.

"Lulabelle!" her father cried, using the pet name he'd called her as a young child. "You're early!"

He jumped down easily from the table and crossed the room to them. She introduced him to Jeff and apologized for being early, explaining that they'd made better time than she'd expected.

"Hey, no *problema*," her father said. "It's just that I have friends staying in my extra room, which I'd planned to let you use. But you can have the couch for tonight. Jeff, are you staying too?"

"No," Jeff answered. He turned to Lula. "It's nearly nine. I'd better get back to face Commander Demento and Terror Pup. I have to deliver the car early tomorrow."

"Okay. If you get shut out, come back here."

Jeff said good-bye to her father and headed for the door. Lula had to fight down the urge to wrap herself around him and cling on for dear life. She thought of little kids who grab their parent by the leg and won't let go while the stiff-legged parent drags the unmovable child around the room. Right then she could totally relate to the separation anxiety those little kids felt. Even though she was with her father, it felt as if Jeff were her real family member.

Jeff had noticed the anxiety in her face. He shot her an encouraging smile and a thumbs-up.

She responded with a tight, worried grin, though she returned the thumbs-up. *Don't leave me here,* she thought as Jeff disappeared out the door.

Rap changed to blasting Latin music, and the partyers formed a conga dance line. Dancing and stumbling on one another, the dancers wiggled their way toward the door.

"Come on, Lula," her father said as he grabbed the waist of the last person in line.

"You go without me," she told him with a halfhearted wave.

She stepped outside and watched the dance line wrap around the pool. She heard the sound of a horn honking and looked to the far end of the pool. A red convertible Cadillac was approaching, jammed with men and women.

Lula clapped her hand to her mouth in horror when she realized that the car wasn't stopping! It had jumped the curb and was heading straight for the pool!

The crowd screamed and scattered.

The car knocked down the wooden fence around the pool and drove straight in. It created a splash that drenched the people on all sides of the pool. The men and women inside laughed as they swam out of the slowly sinking car.

Ruben Cruz had climbed out onto the pool's diving board. "¡Wepa!" he cheered, using the Spanish expression she'd heard him shout before. "Now *this* is a party!"

Lula turned over on her father's couch, further ensnarling her legs in the tropical-print sheet tangled around them. It was almost 3:30 in the morning, but it was impossible to sleep. About six of her father's friends were still hanging out, laughing and drinking, in the open kitchen area.

Her canvas bag, which she'd stashed at the end of the couch, began to ring. She flipped back around, bent forward, and pulled out her cell phone. "Are you okay?" she asked, knowing it had to be Jeff.

"Fine, except I got sent to my room at nine fifteen," he complained.

"That's not so bad. Have you've just been reading or watching TV all this time?" she asked.

"I wish," he grumbled. "It's lights-out at nine thirty! Sharp! If I'd have known, I would have brought a flashlight so I could read under the covers like I used to do at camp."

"Just go to sleep," she suggested.

"I did, for a few hours. But I woke up at two in the morning, and now I can't fall back to sleep!"

"At least you've slept a little. I'm exhausted. The party wound down after somebody called the cops around two thirty," she recalled. "But then they noticed the car in the pool and—"

"The *what* in the *what*?" Jeff interrupted, his voice filled with disbelief.

"I'll tell you about it tomorrow," she promised through a yawn.

"I can't wait," he said.

For a moment or two, they were silent. Then they spoke at once, their voices overlapping. "This is never going to work!"

Three

The cab left Lula off at the corner of Sixth Street and Ocean Drive in front of a large white stucco hotel with deep blue awnings over its many windows. She paid, climbed out, and stood, looking in every direction at the bright, busy world of South Beach.

On the other side of the wide street was a gorgeous sand beach leading to the Atlantic Ocean. It seemed so strange that all she'd have to do was cross the street, pass a sidewalk and a line of low, twisting trees, and she'd be at the beach. In New York City, going to the beach in the summer meant getting on a train or bus, fidgeting restlessly in horrible crowds or traffic jams, and then scrambling for a sliver of red-hot sand to lay your blanket on.

But here—poof!—cross the street and you were at a beach paradise. *How great is that?!* she thought.

Turning, she noticed the cornerstone in the hotel's white stucco. It read: BUILT 1923. Stepping back to see the entire block, she realized that a lot of the hotels, cafés, shops, and restaurants looked as if they had been built in the 1920s and 1930s. She'd read about South Beach's historic Art Deco District in a pamphlet on the trip down.

A woman walked past her dressed in a tiny bikini with a long scarf wrapped around her hips. She turned into a shop a little farther down. Lula had seen many unusual things in New York City—in fact, she saw them on a daily basis—but she couldn't imagine someone just strolling by in a bathing suit—not even a tank suit, never mind the smallest possible bikini!

She suddenly felt way overdressed in her black Capri pants and long-sleeved, oversize white shirt. Although this was what she always wore—she had a winter version that included long pants and a white hooded sweatshirt—it just wasn't right for South Beach.

Two arms wrapped around her from behind, and she jumped. "Save me!" Jeff wailed, hugging her tight. "I've fallen into the clutches of crazy people. My young and beautiful life is now a living hell!"

"Tell me about it," she sympathized. "You want to see crazy people? The party at my father's place never ends. Even when he goes to the nightclub where he bartends, his friends stay behind and keep partying. I haven't slept in days! And I've been living on potato chips and guacamole dip breakfast, lunch, and dinner. That's all he has in the house."

"I'd rather be stuck with party animals than a military moron," Jeff insisted emphatically. "It's like I've been abducted into the army!"

"You mean *inducted*," she corrected him.

"No! I mean *abducted*—as in kidnapped by an alien life force from Mars."

"Mars?" Lula questioned, chuckling.

"Yes, definitely Mars. Wasn't Mars the

Roman god of war or something? Well, that house reminds me of some weird all-military planet. And if you think Uncle Frank was bizarre, wait until you meet Aunt Helen! She just nods and agrees with Uncle Frank like some wife from Stepford."

"Well, I'm really glad to see you, anyway," she said. "Isn't it amazing here?"

"Mad awesome," he agreed. "And look at all these great restaurants. I'm bound to get a job in one of them."

They crossed over to the beach. Taking off their shoes, they walked down to the water's edge. As they stood with their feet in the surf, Jeff suddenly grabbed Lula's wrist. "Look out! Pterodactyl attack!" He shielded his head with his arms as four winged creatures swooped toward them, skimming the water in their search for fish.

"They're pelicans!" Lula said, giving him a playful shove. "Didn't you see *Finding Nemo*?"

Jeff stared after the birds as they flew off, and flashed Lula a grin. "They look different in person. And they don't have Australian accents either!"

"Are you sure? I thought I heard one of

them say, 'G'day, mate,' as he flew by," she said.

They walked along the shoreline, stopping to check out a sand sculpture contest along the way. Someone had built a detailed and huge castle that had won second place. The winner was a mermaid lying on her side. Lula estimated that the sculpture was nearly eight feet long.

After an hour they left the beach and walked down Ocean Drive, just looking at all the shops and restaurants. It was lunchtime, and crowds were filling the outside porches and open-air cafés. A waiter walked past them carrying a platter of clams and shrimp. Jeff stopped to inhale the smell of spices, garlic, and butter. "I'm suddenly starving," he said. "Let's find someplace to eat."

"Someplace cheap," Lula added.

"Not to worry," Jeff said. "I delivered the car and got paid." He took out his wallet and pulled out three hundred dollars. "I'm *filthy* rich."

"That's good, but maybe you should hang on to your money until you get a job," Lula suggested. "Who knows how long it's going to have to last?"

"You're right, but at least let me treat you to lunch," he insisted. "You sort of earned it by taking the ride with me. Besides, you're showing signs of guacamole-and-chip syndrome."

"Oh, yeah?" Lula said with a laugh. "How can you tell?"

"Well, I didn't want to make you self-conscious about it," he replied, "but to tell you the truth, you look a little green, and you're making a crunching sound when you walk. And there's a distinct odor of avocado in the air whenever you're near."

"Ew! Sounds very unattractive," Lula said. "What should I do about it?"

"There's only one cure: grilled shrimp and some kind of drink with pineapple in it. I'm fairly sure we can find that around here somewhere."

They turned up a street called Española Way and admired the Spanish-style stucco buildings. They came to The Clay Hotel, at the corner of Española Way and Washington Street. They sat at an outdoor table shaded by a deep blue umbrella and ordered lunch.

"This is the life," Lula said as she sipped

a piña-colada-flavored smoothie. "Wouldn't it be great if we could just stay here and never go back?"

"Please . . . don't tempt me," Jeff agreed, breathing deeply and looking up at the clear blue sky.

After lunch, they walked around the side streets of South Beach. They poked around in shops that sold clothing, art, books, and gifts.

They bought postcards to send to their friends and family at home. They stopped at another café, ordered lattes, and wrote out their cards. "Today's been the first good time I've had since I got here," Lula said, looking up from her postcard. "I so, *so, so* don't want to go back to my father's place."

"Tell me about it," Jeff agreed.

They finished their cards and continued their stroll around the back streets. As they walked, Lula felt herself becoming depressed. This summer was going to be a total bust. She'd be stuck with a bunch of middle-aged, party-hearty leftovers from the 1970s. She'd have nothing to do until she started school in September. They turned a corner and a sign in front of small restaurant caused them to stop short:

FURNISHED APARTMENT FOR RENT.
INQUIRE WITHIN.

Lula and Jeff stared at each other.

From the look in his suddenly bright eyes, Lula knew she and Jeff were thinking the same thing. "Is it too crazy?" Lula asked.

"It couldn't hurt to take a look," he pointed out.

Pulling open a glass door, they stepped into the dimly lit restaurant. They walked past a desk with a cash register and went down two steps to a room with about ten tables. The tables were set with white clothes and napkins that set off vivid blue plates. But the place seemed empty.

"Hello?" Jeff called.

"Hola," a woman called back in a rich, alto-pitched voice. *"¡Un momento, por favor!"* A swinging kitchen door at the far wall of the room swung open wide, and a heavyset woman in her sixties walked out. Her brisk stride put a jiggle in her wide

curves and caused her full head of dyed r̲e̲
umber hair to bounce.

Her nearly black eyes sparkled, and she
smiled warmly at them. "We are not quite
ready to serve supper yet, but I can find you
a little something to eat. You like *tapas*?
'Tapas' means 'little dishes.' Mexicans serve
tapas, too, but I do them the Cuban way.
¡*Muy bien!* You will love them."

"It sounds delicious," Lula said. "But
we really came to ask about the apartment.
Could we see it?"

"*Sí,* of course!" She took off the white
apron she'd been wearing over a purple
pantsuit. "Come with me."

They followed her through the kitchen
and up a staircase at the very back of it.
"This is a three-story building. There are
two floors of apartments above the restaurant," she explained as they climbed the
dark, narrow stairs. The empty apartment
is on the second floor."

They came out to a green carpeted hallway. The walls were an ocean blue, like so
much else Lula had seen at South Beach.
She liked it. It was certainly better than the
beige-brown hallway walls of her NYC

t building. Jeff had named that
apartment-Complex Brown.

The woman unlocked a door, and they stepped into a small apartment painted a bright lime green. A tiny kitchen of dazzling white cabinets and appliances shared the same space with the living room. "It's nicely furnished," the woman said, pointing to a rattan love seat covered in a bright tropical-patterned fabric. A glass-top coffee table sat in front of it. A small round table with wicker chairs shared the room with everything else.

They stepped into the bedroom, which was painted the same lime green. It had a double bed with a wicker headboard, a small white dresser, and a side table. "There's only one bedroom?" Jeff asked.

The woman raised a questioning eyebrow. "How many do you need?"

"Two would be nice," he answered.

The woman studied them with a puzzled expression, and then she shrugged. "The couch pulls out."

Lula and Jeff looked at each other. It would be cramped. But it was furnished— and it would be theirs.

"What do you think?" Jeff asked Lula.

Lula bit her lip. This was so nuts but . . . "I really want it," she dared to say.

"Me too," he agreed. "Let's do it."

Jeff took out the $278 that was left of his $300 after lunch, and Lula scraped together all the money she had, including the emergency fifty-dollar bill her mother had safety-pinned inside her bag and the change from the bottom of the bag.

It wasn't enough.

"Not to worry," Jeff said. He asked the woman for directions to the nearest ATM. Luckily there was one at a pharmacy just several buildings away.

He pulled a Visa Buxx card from his wallet. "My uncle Tony gave me this when we graduated," he said, keying in his pin number. "I never even looked to see how much money is on this card."

"You never looked?" Lula asked incredulously.

"I wanted it to be a surprise for someday when I really needed the money," he said, punching buttons.

"Only you would think it was fun not

to know how much money you'd received," she commented.

"Sweet!" he cried as the amount came up. "One thousand big ones!"

"What a generous gift!" Lula commented.

"Uncle Tony's loaded," Jeff said. "And yes, it is massively generous. I should have sent him a nicer thank-you card." He took most of the money out of the account, and they rushed back to the apartment, where the woman was sitting on the couch waiting for them.

"Since you are giving me cash, I can wait for a few weeks for the first month's rent," the woman said, counting out the dollars. "My name is CeCe Caracas. I own the restaurant downstairs and I'm your new landlady. Glad to have you."

Lula was so excited, she felt as if she could barely breathe. "Oh-that's-so-great!" she managed to say.

The woman smiled. "I am glad you are glad. I will be right back. I must get an application form."

The moment she left, Jeff and Lula grabbed each other, hopping around the room, giddy with joy. "My uncle will be relieved to be rid of me," Jeff said after they stopped.

"I think my father will be happy too," Lula said. Her words caused a pang of sadness. Her dream of getting to know her father had certainly been a washout. He wasn't a bad guy, she supposed . . . he just wasn't someone who should ever have become a father.

She took out her cell phone and called him. A shiver of excitement ran down her spine. "I should at least tell him I've done this," she said.

No one picked up, and the voice mail came on. "You've reached Ruben Cruz. I'll be away for a couple of days, enjoying myself in sunny Puerto Rico. Call me again later. Lulabelle, honey, got a chance to hop on a cruise ship. See ya in a few days. There's guacamole and chips in the fridge."

Lula clicked off. "He's not home, but I'm fairly positive he'll be just fine with this."

CeCe Caracas returned with the form and a pen. She sat with them at the table while they filled it out together. After about two minutes, someone knocked on the apartment door, which had been left ajar.

They turned toward the door, but before any of them could say a word, a very old man burst in. He was completely bald and wore thick glasses, a large striped shirt, and baggy Bermuda shorts. He set down the large boom box he had been carrying and switched it on.

"Don't worry," Mrs. Caracas assured them in a whisper loud enough to be heard over the music. "It's just dear Mr. Smedlinsky; he lives in an apartment upstairs."

Lula and Jeff stared, goggle-eyed with astonishment, as the man began to dance. The tune was very fast and sounded German or Eastern European. The man, despite his age, did a very lively dance, which involved hopping, kicking, and slapping his knees, head, and even his scrawny rear end. His arms flew wildly from his side with complete abandon.

Mrs. Caracas went to the boom box and hit the Off button.

"No! No!" he protested. He took business cards from his pockets and handed one each to Jeff and Lula. "You learn to dance from Mr. Smedlinsky. I teach."

Lula read the card:

JERZY SMEDLINSKY
I TEACH YOU DANCE
RHUMBA, HIP-HOP, TWIST,
CHA-CHA, POLKA, SLAP DANCE

"Mr. Smedlinsky, no one wants dancing classes right now. *Gracias, pero no,*" CeCe Caracas said. "Besides, usually you give your slap-dancing demonstration down on the beach at this time. You will be late."

With a quick glance at his wristwatch, Mr. Smedlinsky snapped up his boom box and hurried out the door. Mrs. Caracas closed it firmly behind him. "Poor man," she said with a fond smile. "He got involved with a young cage dancer from one of the clubs, and one day she hopped on a Greyhound with his life savings. He was retired, but after she left he had to find work. So now he gives dance lessons."

"What a sad story," Lula said.

"Life is unpredictable," CeCe commented with a knowing nod.

Jeff finished filling out the application form for the two of them and handed it to CeCe. She looked it over. "Your last name is Cruz," she said to Lula. "Did you ever hear the great Cuban singer Celia Cruz?"

"No." Penelope Cruz, the actress, was the only famous Cruz Lula knew of.

"Too bad," CeCe said. "What a talent! I knew her when I was much younger, back in Cuba." She stood with her legs wide. "*¡Azúcar!*" she shouted, making her full hairdo wobble.

Jeff and Lula looked at each other, not sure what to make of this call.

"Celia Cruz was famous for shouting that," CeCe Caracas explained. "She had twenty-two gold albums by the time she died in 2003. *¡Azúcar!* It means sugar."

She went back to reading the application. "You forgot to fill in the part that tells me where you work."

Lula and Jeff looked at each other nervously. What should they say? Would they lose the apartment if they admitted they had no jobs?

"Not working?" Mrs. Caracas asked, picking up on their anxiety.

Lula grimaced and shook her head. "We just got here and we haven't had the chance to—"

"Muy bueno!" Mrs. Caracas cried, grinning widely. "You're hired!"

Lula and Jeff stared at her, not understanding.

"I need a waitress and a cook. You need a job. If you can wait tables or cook, you're hired!" CeCe told Lula.

"I can only cook a little, and I've never waited tables before," Lula admitted. "Jeff's worked in restaurants, though."

Jeff wiggled uncomfortably. "I'm only a prep chef. I only know how to cut and chop and stuff."

"You'll learn the rest," said Mrs. Caracas.

"I don't know," Jeff said hesitantly. "I need a job, but I . . . uh . . . was thinking of something more. . . ."

"You are holding out for a more high-class job," she said, understanding his hesitance.

"Yeah. Since I can't afford chef school, I

was hoping to learn at a real four-star type of restaurant," Jeff said.

"I understand," the woman said. "Okay, you have a few days to find a job. But if you do not find one, I will find you one—right here, with me." She whirled around to Lula. "And you can easily learn to wait tables," she said.

"I can?" Lula questioned. The idea was a little intimidating, but how hard could it be? And it was true that she needed cash, and fast. "Okay," she agreed. "Wow! Just an hour ago I never expected to be living and waiting tables here in South Beach."

Mrs. Caracas wrapped them in a radiant smile. "As I always say: Life is unpredictable. I say it because it's true."

Four

Lula and Jeff took a cab to her father's empty apartment. She packed her bag and left him a note with her new address.

Then they went to Uncle Frank's house—or space station Mars, as Jeff called it—and got Jeff's things. His uncle argued a little but gave in with a look of relief, as Jeff had predicted.

Once again, Terror Pup escorted them to the waiting cab. "That's one demented animal," the driver commented as he raced away.

"We have now spent every last dime we have," Jeff commented as he and Lula pooled the last of their money to pay the driver when they were back at the apartment.

"At least I have a job," Lula said. "And you'll find one soon."

That night Jeff pulled out the couch bed. "You're a girl. You should have the bedroom," he explained.

"Isn't that sort of old-fashioned?" she asked. "I'm surprised you would think like that."

"Hey, I'm gay," he said. "I'm not from another planet. So I have some weird ideas left over from childhood—who doesn't? Take the bedroom. The couch bed is really fine."

"We could switch each night," she suggested.

"I don't want to find all your girl things in my bed," he protested.

Her hands went to her hips. "What girl things?" she demanded.

"Oh, you know—all those secret girl things you girls have," he said.

She realized he was determined to give her the bedroom, and she loved that he was so sweet. She leaned across the bed and kissed his cheeks. "Good night, roommate, and thanks."

"Night, roomie," he called back.

That night she lay in bed, in the hot pink glow of the neon light from the hotel across the street, listening to the constant murmur of the nightlife below and the steady crash of waves. She could hear the ocean clearly even though they were several blocks from the beach. She stretched and pulled down the shade so only a line of pink shone on her covers.

Yawning, she shut her eyes and dreamed of the red convertible that had been driven into the pool at her father's apartment. Only, in the dream, Jeff was driving the car into the pool and she was with him. And the pool became the ocean. The car went down and down and down. She and Jeff panicked, clinging together in the water. Then, suddenly, they realized that they could breathe under water and began to swim around, feeling happier and more free than ever before in their lives.

Lula's alarm rang. With a groan, she snapped open the shade and squinted against the blinding white light pouring in. Once she remembered where she was, she got up and wandered into the cramped, lime green living room, with its tropical furniture. There was a note from Jeff on the table: GONE JOB HUNTING. WISH ME LUCK. JT

Someone rapped on the apartment door. Lula didn't want to answer it wearing only her nightshirt. What if it was Mr. Smedlinsky again? She could never say no to salespeople. If she opened the door, she might be stuck boogying all day with a high-stepping, rump-slapping bald geezer.

The person knocked again, louder this time.

She grabbed Jeff's zip-front sweatshirt that he'd tossed on the couch and she pulled it on over her nightshirt. Then she went to the door, unlocked it, and latched the safety chain. "Who's there?" she asked.

"It's me, Daisy, from upstairs," replied a female voice in a strong British accent.

Lula opened the door a crack and looked out. A stunningly beautiful, very dark-skinned woman of about nineteen or twenty stood in a front of her. She was easily six feet tall, and slender, in cut-off shorts and a halter top. Her black hair was cut close to her head and showed off the row of silver hoops that shimmered in her ears. "Greetings!" she said, lifting up the blender she held. "Care for a drinkie-poo?"

Lula wondered what was in the blender. Surely it wasn't something alcoholic at this time of day. Well, maybe not so surely. The brief time she'd spent with her father had taught her that anything was possible when it came to the way some people liked to party.

"Growing old out here," Daisy prodded her.

Lula opened the door, and Daisy strode in. "Hmm . . . do you actually fancy this lime green on the walls?" she asked doubtfully, looking around. "It could make a person's nerves all jangle-ish, don't you think? A bit too much relentless luminosity, if you ask me."

"I suppose," Lula agreed hesitantly, not really sure how she felt about the bright color. Since she'd come to Miami she'd been struck by the colorful brightness of just about everything.

Daisy opened the kitchen cabinet. The only thing inside was a stack of paper cups and the can of Funk-Off. "We're in luck!" she said, separating the cups and pouring the blender's contents, which turned out to be orange-and-strawberry smoothie, into them. She raised her paper cupful of smoothie in a toast. "Cheers! And here's to ridding yourself of the fungus problem as well."

"Cheers," Lula said, laughing. "There's no fungus problem that we know of. It's just a joke."

Daisy suddenly roared with laughter. "Oh! Funk-Off. Just like we tell someone to sod off."

"That could be a product for removing unwanted grass," Lula joked.

Daisy didn't get it and looked confused. But then she brightened. "Oh, I see . . . sod! Those patches of grass you Americans are so fond of. Brilliant!"

She refilled Lula's cup. "What are you going to be doing here in South Beach?"

Lula told her she would be attending the University of Miami in the fall. "And I'm waiting tables downstairs until the end of the summer."

"At CeCe's?" Daisy asked, sounding

delighted. "How convenient, and you'll just love her!"

"Mrs. Caracas?"

"Yes. CeCe Caracas is just super. She let me have a place even though I came here from England without a pound. I worked for CeCe until I got up enough money to rent my own smoothie stand. Now money's not a problem."

Lula looked at the travel clock she'd set out on the table. It was nearly eleven, and she was expected at the restaurant at noon. She thanked Daisy for the smoothie and told her she had to get ready.

"Ta-ta, then," Daisy said. "I'm so glad we met. I do hope we can be mates. I'll see you on the beach. That's where my stand is located."

The unexpected visit had made Lula feel optimistic and welcome. She quickly dressed in her black Capri pants, one of her white T-shirts, and a pair of black slides.

When she got to the restaurant, it was empty except for a tall, thin man in his thirties. He was setting the table and wore a white apron. His short, perfectly trimmed, receding hair and buttoned-up shirt gave him a neat—even fastidious—appearance. His movements were quick and efficient.

"Hi, I'm Lula Cruz," she introduced herself. "I'm going to start waiting on tables today."

"Shall I alert the *Miami Herald*?" he asked sarcastically.

Lula was about to tell him there was no reason to be rude, when CeCe Caracas burst out of the kitchen, "*Hola,* baby girl!" she greeted Lula. "I see you've met Paulo."

Lula nodded. "Sort of," she said.

"Paulo will show you everything you need to know," she told Lula. She handed Lula a crisp white apron. "He is a wonderful waiter."

"Thanks, Mrs. Caracas," Lula said, fighting down the nervous jitters dancing inside her.

"Now that we know each other, call me CeCe," she said. "Everyone does."

She went back to the kitchen, leaving Lula with Paulo. Since she couldn't catch his eye, she cleared her throat for his attention.

"Hot sauce, one on each table," he told

her, still not looking at her. "Over there, and combine any that are half full."

She found the small bottles of red sauce and began distributing them. Then she went back to the kitchen to combine the halves.

CeCe was hacking chicken pieces apart with a small cleaver. "You know Cuban food?" she asked Lula.

"No. I'm part Puerto Rican," Lula replied. "Part Irish."

"Puerto Rican and Cuban food are different in some ways, the same in others," she said. "To tell you the truth, I'm not really a cook. My husband was the chef, but he passed on last year."

"I'm sorry," Lula said.

CeCe sighed. "Me too. He was a wonderful man—and a fabulous cook. Unfortunately, I didn't learn anything about cooking from him. But I try my best. I could really use someone to take over the cooking in here."

This might be the perfect place for Jeff to learn, Lula thought. And it would be great to have him to laugh with. She couldn't imagine herself doing much laughing with the stern-faced, sarcastic Paulo out there.

Lula went back out with the new bottles of hot sauce and continued placing them on tables. Before long a man and woman came in. Paulo jerked his head toward them, motioning for Lula to take their order.

She hurried over to the middle-aged couple. The man wore an obvious toupee and lots of gold chains. The woman was in a too tight red dress, her ample cleavage heaving forward at the neckline.

"Welcome to CeCe's Cuban Café," Lula greeted them. "Can I take your orders?"

"We need menus," the man said in an annoyed tone.

"Yes! That might help," the woman added sarcastically.

"Oh! Of course." Lula ran up to Paulo. "Do we have menus?"

"No, we just hope our customers can guess what we have," he answered dryly.

Lula sighed, angry at herself for asking such a dumb question. "I mean, where *are* the menus?"

Paulo pointed to a slate with the day's offerings written on it:

ROPA VIEJA (SHREDDED BEEF)
GARLIC ROASTED CHICKEN
ARROZ CON POLLO (CHICKEN WITH RICE)
HAMBURGUESA CUBANA (CUBAN HAMBURGER)

Lula realized she didn't have a pad, but how difficult could it be to remember their orders?

Another couple came in, and Paulo waited on them. He and Lula both arrived in the kitchen together and gave CeCe the orders.

Lula then went back out to bring the couple their drinks. She had to go back and change them because she had accidentally switched the diet with the regular Coke.

She grabbed the two plates of food that CeCe had put up on the serving shelf in the kitchen, and then hurried out with them. "Here you go," Lula said, setting down the plates.

"This is not *arroz con pollo*," the woman said, pushing the plate away.

"I'm sure you ordered chicken," Lula said, confused.

"I ordered *arroz*—rice—too!" she replied angrily. "Do you see rice on this plate?"

"No. Sorry," Lula said, scooping up the plate and hurrying back to the kitchen with it.

"There's my roasted chicken," Paulo said. He exchanged the plate of *arroz con pollo* he was holding for her roasted chicken, and she rushed back to the table with it. She was moving so fast, she didn't notice the black bean that had slipped off the plate and onto the floor.

"Yaaaiiiyyy!" She slid along the wooden floor, the bean skidding along under her heel. Trying desperately to keep her plate up, Lula realized she was headed straight for her customers.

She hit the table, sending the chicken wing, rice, and black beans high into the air. Cokes splashed as she fell backward onto the floor.

The roasted chicken wing banged down on the man's head, knocking his hairpiece to the side. The chicken wing then bounced up off his bald head and landed right down the front of the woman's dress, clenched in place by her Wonderbra.

"I'm so sorry," Lula cried as she climbed up off the floor.

With one hand on his fake hair, the man stormed out. His date yanked the chicken from her bosom and hurled it at Lula before joining him.

CeCe had run out of the kitchen to see what was happening. Paulo was beside her, holding the two meals he had been about to deliver.

Lula hurried up to them, shaking and covered with soda. "I'm so, so sorry!" she said.

Paulo turned to CeCe. "Now do you believe me?" he asked her.

"Okay, you win," CeCe replied. "I guess it's true. . . . My chicken is a little rubbery."

Paulo scowled. "A little rubbery? That chicken bounced farther than Serena Williams's best serve."

"Okay, so what if your first day at work will someday be made into a disaster movie starring Ashton Kutcher and Hilary Duff?" Jeff said later that day. It was about six o'clock, and they were walking along Ocean Drive on the beach side. "At least she didn't fire you."

"I think she was afraid to come too

close to me," Lula replied. "She was probably afraid she'd be sucked into the black
hole of disaster that I had become. It didn't
stop all day. I spilled things. I got orders
mixed up. I even forgot to give someone
the check and they left without paying."

Jeff chuckled. "At least you *have* a job.
I got laughed out of some of the best
restaurants in SoBe today."

"SoBe?" she asked.

"Yes. That what those of us who are in
the know call South Beach," he explained.
"And now *you* know what those in the
know know, ya know?"

"I guess I know," she agreed, laughing.

They stopped in front of a clothing
store. "This place sells bathing suits," he
pointed out.

Despite all her mishaps, Lula had
earned thirty dollars in tips at lunch. She
had no bathing suit, so she and Jeff were
now on a mission to find one for her.

"Remember," he said as he pulled open
the door to the store. "Don't pick out
something that says 'Mother Teresa at the
seashore' all over it."

"I'm not the type of girl who has to

show everything I've got," she insisted.

"No kidding," he agreed. "I'm still in shock from your last bathing suit."

"You mean that cute suit with the knee-length board shorts and short-sleeved top?"

"That's the one," he replied. "The only thing missing was the little ruffled swim bonnet."

"I would have packed that suit but I could never find it again after that day I wore it to Coney Island with you."

"I have a confession," he said. "You couldn't find it because I threw it in the incinerator. I saw it on a chair in your apartment one day and just thought, *What the heck. She'll thank me someday.* After all, what are gay guy friends for, if not to save you from your worst fashion mistakes?"

"You burned my bathing suit?" Lula cried, aghast.

"It's not like I made a bonfire and danced around it or anything. I just dumped it down the incinerator chute."

"I can't believe you burned it," she said again. "Did you really? Are you telling me the truth?"

"Yes, and, not to worry, that's why I'm generously offering to help you pick out a new one—a much better one," he said, guiding her into the store. "Someday when I'm *filthy rich* again, I'll even offer to pay for it."

Inside, Lula looked through a rack of Speedo tank suits, while Jeff brought over bikinis he thought would look good on her. After she refused the tenth bikini offering, he gave up. "You're hopeless," he told her. "I'm going to go look in the men's department."

"Happy hunting," she said as he wandered off. She pushed a few more suits down the rack and picked one out, but she couldn't keep her mind on shopping. Maybe Jeff was right. It was possible that her style needed a little shaking up. She realized she was holding a black tank suit in her hand.

She put it back and went over to the two-piece rack. Pushing aside a group of hot pink and lime green string bikinis, she looked for something with a little more coverage.

After trying on four suits, she settled on

a denim fabric two-piece with a halter top and board shorts.

"Perfect," Jeff said, appearing from behind a rack. "I'm proud of you for showing your *girlage* a little." He came alongside her and leaned in close. "Don't be obvious," he said in a low tone. "But shift your drift to the right by the flip-flops over there."

Lula pretended to stretch and casually glanced to the right. She froze mid stretch.

Standing in front of the flip-flops rack was the hottest hottie she'd ever laid eyes on. He was about six feet tall, maybe a little taller. Broad shoulders muscled out from under a black T-shirt. His jeans weren't too tight, but were tight enough to give a truly inspiring rear view. "Whoa," she breathed out, letting her arms drop.

He turned their way as though sensing the attention they'd focused on him. Large dark eyes took them in, and his white teeth glinted slightly when he smiled at them.

Both Jeff and Lula smiled back, dazed and confused by the brilliance of his looks. *We must look like two escapees from the psycho ward,* Lula realized.

Despite that, she couldn't stop staring at him as he walked away from the flip-flops to the front counter.

"Did you see how he was totally checking me out?" Jeff whispered.

"Dream on," Lula disagreed. "He was smiling at me."

"Uh-uh," Jeff insisted. "Gay all the way."

Lula watched him head toward the front door and—just before he walked out the door—he stopped and looked over at them.

He was interested in . . . one of them. *Be straight, be straight, please be straight,* she found herself feverishly hoping as she went back to the rack and reconsidered the hot pink string bikini.

Five

"What good is getting a sexy suit if you're going to wear the world's biggest T-shirt at all times?" Jeff asked as they left Ocean Drive and strolled along the beach's cement walkway a few days later.

"All right! All right!" Lula cried. Yanking off her oversize T-shirt, she scowled at Jeff. She turned in a circle, showing off the skimpy hot pink bikini. "There! Are you happy?"

"You look great. I'd be even happier if you'd lose the glasses," he replied.

"Can you tell me why you want to see me stumbling around the beach, half naked and nearly blind!" she grumbled.

"You don't have to be blind. You know you could wear your contacts," he countered. "You have them, so why don't you use them?"

"They make my eyes feel dry."

"They do not. You just never gave them a chance," he insisted. "Your eyes are awesome! Why do you want to hide them behind glasses?"

Lula suddenly sat down on a bench set back off the walkway. "Why are you picking on me today?" she asked.

"I'm not," he insisted with an edge of annoyance, but then he softened and sat down beside her. "Am I? I don't mean to. It's just that it seems as if you hide behind those big shirts and beach cover-ups and your glasses. And sometimes I think you even . . ." He stopped himself, deciding not to say what had been on the tip of his tongue.

"What?" she demanded.

"Well, maybe you hide behind me, too," he added.

"I do not!" she cried indignantly.

"Lula, you only dated two guys all through high school, and only for a few months each," he reminded her.

"They weren't any fun. I always had more fun hanging with you," she said.

"But we even went to the prom together."

"I had fun at the prom," she said. "I thought you did too."

"I did, but . . ." He sighed, seeming to run out of steam and not finding the words for what he wanted to express. "It *was* a fun night."

Three good-looking guys in their twenties were walking along the path toward them. Jeff waved, and they waved back. "That's Marc, Jon, and Ethan," he told her. "They share the apartment upstairs—the big one next to Daisy."

"Yours?" she guessed.

"Totally," he answered. "Marc, the cute one with the long blond hair, is a costume designer for a gay theater group. Jon, the one who looks like Adam Sandler, is a psych student at University of Miami, and the last guy, Ethan, the skinny one, is writing a screenplay. Nice guys." He stood up and took a step toward them. "I'm going to go say hi. Come and meet them."

Lula stayed seated. "I'll be there in a

minute. You go." Really, she would have loved to meet them. But she was thinking about what Jeff had just said: that she hid behind him. Maybe it was true, in a way. And what if he was feeling that he needed some space from her? People always assumed they were a couple, and that could be making it difficult for him to meet other guys, even if it was just as friends.

He took a step to leave but stopped. "You okay?" he asked.

"Yep. Catch you later." He still seemed hesitant about leaving, so she got up and, with a wave, sauntered off along the walkway just beyond the trees and benches. She passed two men who looked her over with long, lingering glances. She hurried away and, when they were no longer staring, put the T-shirt back on.

She spied Daisy at her smoothie stand, with its gleaming metal cart and cheerful yellow umbrella, and hurried toward her. It was great to see a friendly face when she was suddenly feeling so all alone.

"Oh, thank god you're here!" Daisy greeted her. "I am dying to go to the loo!"

Lula looked at her quizzically. "The loo?"

"The WC, the water closet! The little girls' room!" Daisy explained.

"Oh! Sure! Go!" Lula told her. "I'll watch the stand."

"Thanks," Daisy said. "I'm sure no one will come. It's been slow as snails all day. And if someone does come by, just say I'll be back."

"I can handle it," Lula assured her. How hard could it be to make a smoothie?

Daisy rushed off, and Lula stepped behind the cart. She watched the people walking by, wondering what each of them did and why they'd come to South Beach. Everything was so different from New York City. Maybe she'd try to get over to the university soon and check out the—

"Excuse me." A voice pulled her out of her reverie.

Lula turned and froze.

It was him—the amazing hottie they'd seen in the store!

"Could I get a Tropical Kiss?"

"Huh?" Lula said, too surprised by his unexpected appearance to think straight. Had he really said he wanted a kiss? She must be dreaming!

Lula felt something like lightning zap back and forth between them. The sensation lasted a second, but it felt so real, not at all like something she'd imagined.

"A Tropical Kiss," he repeated, pointing to the sign on the front of the cart. "A coconut-strawberry-kiwi-pineapple smoothie."

"Oh!" Lula said, laughing nervously. "I thought you said a tropical *fish.* I didn't hear you correctly."

Well, that was pretty lame of me, she thought. But she'd felt she had to say *something* to explain her dazed slowness to react. "You want a smoothie," she continued, desperately stalling until her brain could return from wherever it had disappeared to. "Sure. Sure thing."

God! He was gorgeous! Now that she saw him up close he was even more insanely handsome than she'd thought. His olive skin was perfectly tanned. He even *smelled* delicious, like coconut and almond sunscreen.

He took off his sunglasses and cleaned them on his white linen shirt. Looking up, he smiled at her. Just as they had when she first saw him, his whiter than white teeth glinted in the sun. Unbelievable brown eyes sparkled at her, and she noticed they were flecked with green and gold and rimmed with thick black lashes.

All at once she was glad she'd put her big T-shirt back on and, at the same time, wished she hadn't. At least she could take off her glasses and hope that Jeff was right about her eyes being amazing. So what if she couldn't see his face as well as before? It was a face she wasn't likely to forget.

"One Tropical Kiss coming up," she said, removing her glasses with what she hoped was a casual gesture, as if one always removed one's glasses before concocting a mixed beverage.

The trick now was seeing the ingredients inside the cart without her glasses. It shouldn't be too hard. Pineapple was yellow, strawberry was red, kiwi was green, and coconut was white. The frozen yogurt was cold. She could feel her way to it. She could manage this.

"Didn't I see you in a store a few days ago?" he asked.

Yes! she cheered inwardly. He'd remembered seeing *her.* He'd recalled *her*—not Jeff. He was straight!

"You were looking at bathing suits," he reminded her.

"Oh yes, now I remember," she said, working hard to seem cool. She put the ingredients into the blender. "I was with a friend of mine." She hoped he'd picked up on the way she'd said *friend.* Not a boyfriend, just a *friend.*

"Oh, I didn't notice your friend," he said, "but I remember seeing you. Did you find anything you liked?"

Liked? Did he know how much she liked him? Was she that obvious? Then she realized what he'd meant. "Oh, you mean a bathing suit. Yes, I found one I liked."

She tossed all the ingredients into the blender and hit the button.

Smoothie goop instantly sprayed and splattered everywhere! She'd forgotten to put the top on before hitting the button!

Blindly, she pounded on the blender's controls as the two of them were pelted with cold, sticky smoothie. She hit it frantically but couldn't find the Off button.

The smoothie shot into her hair and on her T-shirt. And it was all *over* him. Even without her glasses, she could see that much!

"Gaw!" Daisy cried, running back toward them. "What's going on?"

"You're back! Great," Lula cried, wanting only to disappear. "Sorry about the mess."

Daisy punched the Off button, and the smoothie storm whirred to a halt. Daisy burst into peals of laughter. "The two of you look such a fright!"

Mystery hottie stood there, his arms extended from his sides, dripping smoothie.

"Yeah, sorry about . . . it all," Lula apologized to him. There was no salvaging this disaster. She just had to get out of this mortifying scene instantly. "See ya!"

Avoiding the blurry shapes along the walkway, she ran toward the sidewalk. When she got there, she hurried back toward her apartment, leaving a trail of pink smoothie footprints on the sidewalk as she went.

Six

That night Lula worked the dinner shift at CeCe's. "Getting better," Paulo commented at the end of the night. He shot her a tight, quick smile, which was the most warmth she'd ever seen from him. Lula assumed he was referring to the fact that she hadn't dumped a meal on anyone's head that night and had only totally botched one order.

She actually thought it was pretty amazing that she'd done well during dinner. She was still unstrung by the blender incident. Added to that, she was trying to adjust to her contact lenses. During the smoothie explosion she'd forgotten about her glasses and left them behind at the cart.

Before going to her place she headed up to Daisy's apartment to see if Daisy had found her glasses.

It was eleven o'clock, but music was blasting from the apartment down the hall. When she knocked on Daisy's door, Mr. Smedlinsky stuck his bald head out the door. "You learn dance with Mr. Smedlinsky?"

"Uh . . . no, but thank you, Mr. Smedlinsky," she said, trying to decline as politely as possible. "I just finished work and my feet are really throbbing. I've been on them all—"

Before she could finish her sentence, Mr. Smedlinsky leaped into the hall and extended his hand gallantly. Unable to decline when faced with his sparkly blue eyes, she took it. Instantly she was swept down the hall, dancing a wild polka.

She'd learned to polka in gym class, but she could barely keep up with the spry old man. They danced down the hall and then back up again.

They were by Daisy's door again when Mr. Smedlinsky finished his dance by spinning Lula out of his arms. She was still spinning when Daisy opened the door, allowing Lula to spin right into the apartment.

"Now that's what I call an entrance!" Daisy remarked. She shut the door, and seconds later Mr. Smedlinsky's business card came sliding under it.

Lula picked it up. The words "I teach" were underlined. "Thanks for the dance, Mr. Smedlinsky," Lula called through the wall. She wasn't sure if he could hear her over the music still blasting on his boom box.

"He's always doing that to me, too," Daisy said, laughing. "It's usually kind of fun, but a bit alarming if you're not expecting him."

"I came to apologize about today," Lula said once Daisy and she had stopped laughing.

"Oh, yeah," Daisy cried, and began laughing again. "What a mess-up! The poor fella was even more covered in smoothie than you were. But good lord, wasn't he gorgeous? Did you snog him?"

"What?" Lula cried. She had no idea what Daisy meant, but it sounded dirty.

"Snog! Snog!" Daisy said excitedly.

"What are you talking about?" Lula asked.

"What are you, daft or something?" she asked. "I'm talking about kissing!"

"Ooooooh!" Lula cried, finally understanding. "Is that what you say in England?"

"Yeah, among other things," Daisy confirmed. "I thought maybe you got the chance to lick some smoothie from Mr. Gorgeous's lips."

"I would have loved to!" Lula admitted, "That's why I took off my glasses, although it didn't turn out the way I'd hoped!"

Daisy screamed with laughter. "I don't blame you for being gaga," she gasped. "You cheeky little devil! But you're not alone. All the girls are mad about him."

"He *is* straight, then?" Lula asked.

"Are you joking? He's like the straight sex god of Ocean Drive. He sings at one of the restaurants, and I hear the place is packed with girls every night."

"Oh," Lula said, disappointed. What chance did she have with the sex god of Ocean Drive?

"Don't look so glum," Daisy said. "I don't think he has a steady girlfriend or anything like that. You have as good a shot at him as anyone."

In theory, that might be true, Lula thought, but it wasn't every girl who had pelted him with rapid-fire blasts of smoothie mix. Most likely that put her pretty far back in the race for his affections. "You didn't find my glasses, did you?" Lula asked, wanting to change the subject.

Daisy shook her head. "Forget about the glasses. You look so much better without them." She walked behind Lula. "Yes, there it is. I thought so," she said. "You even have a gorgeous J.Lo butt."

Suddenly self-conscious, Lula clapped her hands on her behind. She'd always thought her butt was a little too large. She'd never considered it an asset.

Jeff knocked on the door and Daisy let him in. "The guys and I are going to watch an old Hitchcock flick—*The Birds*," he told them. "We could hear you talking from next door and thought you might like to come watch it with us?"

Daisy shivered. "Ooooh, I just adore

The Birds. It's so horrifically creepy!"

Lula and Daisy joined Marc, Jon, and Ethan next door. Lula thought each of them seemed interesting in his own way.

"Jeff says you're a poet," Ethan said as he pulled a chair up to the TV for Lula.

"I've only had things published in little journals and in the school literary magazine," she replied.

"She's awesome," Jeff jumped in. "She's going to the University of Miami on a writing scholarship."

"Nice!" said Jon. "I can show you around in the fall. I'm in my last year there."

"Jon's a psych major. He can analyze you too," Daisy said, curling up at the end of the couch. "He says I have issues with men because my father was emotionally distant."

"My father is very warm but totally unreliable," Lula revealed.

"That will give you issues," Jon said as he took the bag of popcorn from the microwave. "Different ones from Daisy's, but issues just the same."

"Lula avoids getting romantically involved," Jeff pointed out. Lula shot him a glare.

"Well, you *do*," he insisted.

"That could definitely be a result of having an unreliable father," Jon confirmed.

"Leave the poor girl alone and watch the movie," Marc told them. The old Hitchcock film had begun. The beautiful, blond actress Tippi Hedren was putting a cage with two lovebirds into the car. "Look at that outfit she's wearing. They really knew how to dress in 1963," he remarked.

"I never really understand what's going on in this movie," Lula admitted. "I know the birds attack, but why?"

"It's more of a psychological study," Ethan suggested.

"Absolutely," Jon agreed. "The birds reflect the psychological chaos going on inside Tippi Hedren's character."

They watched the old Hitchcock thriller, and Lula had never seen it before in quite the same way. Ethan, who was writing his own screenplay, kept pointing out the clues and hidden meanings in the story. Marc was enthralled by the costumes and knew so much about clothing. And Jon gave insights into the psychology of the characters.

It was after two in the morning before

Lula and Jeff returned to their apartment. "I told you they were good guys," Jeff said as he pulled out the couch. "Daisy's cool too."

Lula remembered that she hadn't had a chance to tell him all about her total humiliation at the beach. But she was exhausted and really didn't want to relive it, anyway. "I'll take the couch tonight," she offered.

"Nope," he declined, kicking off his shoes. "I told you, you can have the room. I really don't mind."

"Thanks," she said, yawning. She went into her room and changed into her night-shirt. Crawling into bed, she tossed and turned and couldn't seem to settle down to sleep.

She kept thinking about the guy at the beach. She didn't even know his name—but somehow she felt connected to him. She'd felt it that first day in the store.

So many thoughts and feelings raced through her. Even though she had absolutely no chance with the mystery hottie, she couldn't stop thinking about him. There would be no way she could fall asleep

before writing some of her feelings down as
a poem. Pulling her small notebook and a
pen from the top drawer of the rattan night
stand, she began to write.

Electric Storm
By Lula Cruz

Zap. Flash.
Quicksilver electric connection.
I have never seen
Anything like you.
Heart smash. Mind crash.
Flowing in your direction.
I have never felt
Anything like you.

Seven

"If I don't find a job soon, Mrs. Caracas is going to make me work for her," Jeff said. It was nearly four o'clock in the afternoon, and Lula and he were headed for the beach.

Lula had just finished working the lunch shift, and Jeff had spent another day searching, unsuccessfully, for a job. "She can't *make* you work for her," she reminded Jeff.

"Mrs. Caracas is the most charming and persuasive person I have ever met," Jeff said. "Could you say no to her?"

Lula laughed because what he said was true. "Probably not," she admitted.

Down on the beach, they could see Mr.

Smedlinsky, dressed only in baggy swim trunks. Accompanied by his boom box, he was doing something that resembled hip-hop dancing. "You could always go teach dancing with Mr. Smedlinsky," Lula teased. "He seems to be drawing quite a crowd."

Jeff gazed at their neighbor as he hip-hopped before an ever-growing group of people. "If Mr. S. starts spinning on his head, I'm outta here," he commented.

"Seriously, though," Lula said, laughing. "CeCe could really use you in the kitchen. She's a terrible cook, which is probably why business is so bad. I only made twenty dollars in tips today. Paulo only made thirty."

"What's the story on that guy?" Jeff asked. "He's gay, right?"

"I don't know," she replied. "We don't ever chat."

"He's gay," Jeff said confidently. "You can just tell by looking at him, by the way he *is*."

"Stereotype," Lula warned. "You thought the guy in the store was gay, but you were wrong."

"True," Jeff conceded, "but that was

just wishful thinking. Some guys fit the gay male stereotype, and Paulo does. The other day when I walked through the restaurant, he was rearranging the paintings on the walls."

"Stereotype," Lula insisted.

"Educated guess," Jeff countered. He dug in the back pocket of his shorts and pulled out a flyer. "I almost forgot! I found this today while I was out shamelessly begging for employment all over Miami."

Lula took the paper from him. "Shut up! No way! This is unbelievable!" The paper announced that her all-time-favorite poet, her absolute idol, Nzoake Jones, would be reading her poetry at the University of Miami next week.

She took out her cell phone and immediately called the number on the flyer to get tickets. "Noooooo," she wailed when she learned the reading was sold out.

"What a bust," Jeff sympathized.

"I can't believe she's going to be right here and I won't get to see her," Lula said.

Jeff clutched Lula's wrist. "Look who's heading our way," she said in an urgent tone.

Lula followed his gaze. "Oh, no!" It was *him*! Mystery Hottie! She turned to Jeff, panicked. "I ruined that expensive white linen shirt he was wearing yesterday!"

"How do you know it was expensive?" Jeff asked

"It looked like it was." She wrung her hands. "He's probably furious. What if he wants me to buy him a new one? I can't afford to pay for a shirt like that." The tips were so bad at CeCe's that she couldn't even pay the rent, never mind paying for a man's linen shirt.

And there was no doubt that he was walking *directly* toward them!

"Lula, maybe he just wants to . . . ," Jeff began. It didn't matter. Lula had ducked behind a tremendously fat woman and was sneaking off, hiding behind her.

The oversize woman scowled at Lula, who smiled sheepishly back at her. "Don't mind me," Lula said with a nervous chuckle. "I thought you were someone I know— which I see you're not. You don't mind if I walk with you for a while, do you?"

"Buzz off!" the woman shouted, giving Lula a shove that sent her sprawling onto the sand. Getting to her feet, she saw Mystery Hottie speaking to Jeff. Jeff was shrugging his shoulders, but then Mystery Hottie spotted her and began to run in her direction.

Panic lit a spark under Lula's heels, and she dashed away from him. Her feet pounded the burning sand as she fled.

Out on the sidewalk she darted between two parked cars and crossed busy Ocean Drive. She saw him cross a few yards away. He signaled to her, but she kept going, desperate to escape him. Not only was she unable to pay for his ruined shirt, she was also completely mortified—beyond humiliated!—by what had happened. She couldn't possibly face him.

The two of them weaved in and out of the crowds on the street as Lula ran and Mystery Hottie pursued. He was going to catch up with her soon. Realizing how fast and athletic he was made her more attracted to him than ever—but she couldn't think about that now.

Focus! she commanded herself. He'd catch her in a minute if she didn't do something.

Lula ducked onto the covered outside deck of a crowded café. Had he seen where she went? She turned to check over her shoulder. He was gone—she'd gotten away from him.

With a relieved sigh, she turned to leave and smacked right into a wall of chest—a waiter carrying a tray with salsa, chips, and a pitcher of sangria above his shoulder. At least it *had* been perched at shoulder level before she'd crashed into him and sent the tray and its contents careening down on top of her.

The pitcher was plastic and didn't hurt too much when it hit her. But she was covered with red liquid, fruit, chips, and salsa. "Oh!" he sputtered. "Oh!"

In the next moment, Mystery Hottie bounded up onto the deck. Almost immediately, he slipped on the salsa covering the floor.

He slid into Lula as she attempted to get up and knocked her down again. Clutching at a tablecloth, he pulled it down—along with all the dishes, plates, and utensils on it—before landing on the floor beside her.

Everyone on the deck laughed and applauded. Lula could feel her cheeks burning red with embarrassment.

"We can't keep meeting like this," Mystery Hottie said. He got to his feet and offered his hand to help her up. "Are you all right?"

She nodded but was too mortified to even look at him. "I think I prefer you in tropical smoothie," he joked. "Salsa and sangria aren't really your colors."

He took her eyeglasses from his shirt pocket. "I was trying to return these to you," he explained, handing them to her. "You ran off and forgot them yesterday."

How could this possibly have happened two days in a row?! Was she jinxed? Cursed?

A squad of bus boys and girls ran out to clean up the mess. Once again, the customers began to applaud.

It was all too embarrassing! Lula mumbled her thanks and, clutching her glasses, ran from the deck.

Lula had showered and was watching TV by the time Jeff came in. "It happened," he announced grimly. "She snagged me on the way up the stairs."

"Hmm?" Lula said, looking away from the MTV video she'd been watching. "Who got you?"

"Mrs. Caracas," he explained.

"She said life was unpredictable and maybe I'd find the job of my dreams soon," he related. "But—until that happy day—she would employ me in her kitchen."

"Great," Lula said. "It's perfect, really. You want to cook. She needs a cook. You need a job. She has a job to give you. And we'll be working together. It'll be a blast."

"But all I've ever done was chop and slice the stuff the cooks and chefs gave to me to chop and slice. Garnishing plates with sprigs of parsley is about as high level as I ever got. I don't know recipes, and I especially don't know anything about Cuban cooking," he replied.

Lula considered this. "I know a little about Puerto Rican cooking from my *abuela*." Her grandmother had stayed in her life, even after her father had taken off for Florida. She lived only three blocks away, and Lula had spent a lot of time in her kitchen while she cooked. Even though Lula had never tried to make any of her *abuela*'s delicious Puerto Rican recipes, she'd watched her prepare them.

"The secret ingredient in Puerto Rican cooking is the *recaito,* which is made from *recao* or cilantro, onions, garlic, and peppers—all blended up together. Or you could use *sofrito,* which is almost the same thing, only *Abuela* added tomatoes to it before she used it. Just throw that in everything—especially your beans—put banana-kind-of-fruits called plantains on the side, and you can't miss."

"But this is Cuban cooking, not Puerto Rican," Jeff reminded her.

Lula shrugged. "CeCe said the two are the same in a lot of ways. She told me the other day that Cuban dishes combine a lot of different styles of cooking from South America, North America, and even Africa. Besides, whatever you make has got to be better than what *she* cooks. Yesterday I dropped a plate of her black beans on the floor and when I went to clean it up, the varnish came off, too."

"That can't be good," Jeff remarked, cringing at the thought.

"Definitely not good," Lula agreed. She pointed the remote control at the TV and switched to The Food Network. A woman was showing how to make a beef stew. "I'm telling you, make that, throw some beans with *recaito* or *sofrito* into it, and call it Cuban. No one will know the diff. Goya even makes frozen *recaito* and *sofrito*. My mother used to use it when she tried to cook Puerto Rican."

"It sounds easy when *you* say it," Jeff admitted. "But I've never cooked in a restaurant before. I've never actually created the recipes or cooked anything."

"Then this a great chance for you," Lula pointed out. "It's a priceless opportunity."

"Yeah, maybe so," Jeff agreed, his optimistic nature starting to gain the upper hand. "Hey, did Mr. Wonderful ever catch up with you?"

"He did."

"Did he ask you to pay for his shirt?"

"No, he returned my glasses," Lula said, and went on to tell him the whole humiliating story. By the time she had finished, he was doubled over, breathless with laughter.

"It wasn't funny," Lula insisted, although she couldn't suppress a smile. Maybe it was a *little* funny—if it had happened to someone else.

"It's hot in here," Jeff said, getting up to open a window and let in the night air. "There's no air-conditioning in here, is there?"

"As soon as we get some money, we'd better get a window unit," Lula said. "Feel like taking a walk?"

"Sure," Jeff agreed. "It's my last night as a free man. After tonight, I become an indentured servant to Mrs. Caracas."

"Call her CeCe," Lula told him as she slipped into her new flip-flops with the half-inch heel. "She's really great. You'll like her."

They walked around the corner and up Española Way to Ocean Drive. The street was packed with both locals and tourists. Neon signs lit the night and illuminated the wild mix of people. Gorgeously dressed nightclubbers stepped out of limos and walked along the crowded street with rowdy partyers still in their bathing suits.

On one corner, a man dressed in only cut-off jeans was demonstrating tai chi moves. Farther down the block, two young women who were obviously twins balanced chairs on their chins and passed a hat for donations. As Lula and Jeff mingled with the passersby, every few yards presented them with something new to see. Music spilled out of the many cafés, restaurants, and clubs, combining with the sound of crashing surf from the ocean across the street.

They stopped in front of a café called La Bamba. Throbbing Latin music blasted out every time someone went in or out. Lula couldn't help moving to the beat. "Let's go in," she suggested. "I have enough money to split an appetizer and buy us two iced teas."

"Okay," Jeff agreed.

As soon as they stepped inside the glass doors, the music stopped. "We'll be back after a real quick break," a male voice told the audience.

Lula made a disappointed face. "Too bad."

They found a seat near the stage area and ordered two iced mango teas, and a plate of nachos with refried beans, jalapeño peppers, and cheese. Lula suddenly drew in a sharp breath. "He's here!" she said with a sharp gasp. Mystery Hottie was walking toward the table. "I can't face him," she said as she slowly sank down in her chair until she disappeared under the table.

The waiter came with their order. Looking down, he saw Lula under the table. "Lose something?" he asked.

"Uh, no," she replied, not willing to get up. Lula had the feeling she'd seen the waiter somewhere before. "Do I know you?" she asked, still crouched under the table.

"Picture me covered with salsa and sangria," he suggested. "That might give you a clue."

Lula cringed and realized he was the same waiter she'd smashed into that afternoon. In fact, this was the same place. "Sorry about that," she whispered.

"Yes, well, care to join the rest of us?" he asked.

"Not really," she replied.

From under the table she could see Mystery Hottie's khaki pants and sandals. He was almost beside them.

The waiter put the food and drinks down. "Would you please ask your friend to get up?" he asked Jeff.

"She will," he replied. "Sometime soon."

Lula stared at Mystery Hottie's feet. Why wouldn't he leave? He was probably wondering where she'd disappeared to. Maybe he planned to wait for her there. What was she going to do? She had to find a way to get out of there. Well, she couldn't stay there all night. She'd just have to face him.

"Found it!" she said in a voice that was just a little too loud. She rose and pretended to have something stuck to her index finger. "It's so hard to find those darn contact lenses when they fall on the floor. Luckily, I found the one that fell out, though."

Looking around, she didn't see Mystery Hottie. He hadn't heard a word of her big excuse. Jeff nodded toward the stage.

He stood there holding a microphone.

"We're back," he told the crowd as the band behind him assembled. "In case you just came in, I'm Enrique Reyes. The band is the Miami Hombres, and we'd like to do a song called 'Sin Ella.'"

"That means 'Without Her,'" Lula told Jeff.

"Duh! I know that much Spanish," he replied.

The band began to play with a hot salsa sound. Mystery Hottie—whose name she now knew was Enrique—sang in Spanish. What a voice! Smooth and powerful!

Remembering what Daisy had told her, she checked the audience. Daisy hadn't been kidding! Tables of gorgeous young women sat staring up at him, completely enthralled.

Enrique began to move to the beat as he sang. "Oh, god, why couldn't he be gay?" Jeff commented longingly.

Lula crumpled the napkin at her place. How could she have fallen so hard for someone so . . . obviously gorgeous? Why did it have to be someone every other female in South Beach was after? And why did she have to go slobber food all over him both times she'd had the chance to talk to him? "I want to go," she told Jeff. "Please."

He seemed hesitant to leave, but gave in.

"Why did you want to leave?" he asked when they were outside.

"I couldn't stand thinking about how hopeless it all is," she admitted to Jeff as she began walking back toward their apartment. "I'm so stuck on that guy!"

"Who wouldn't be?" Jeff sympathized, following along. Then he stopped, staring at Lula in surprise. "Man, you really *are* into him. What's going on?"

"I don't know! This is so unlike me," she agreed.

"Want me to squirt him with Funk-Off?" he offered.

"You might have to," she said.

When they arrived back at the apartment, Jeff checked the messages on his cell phone. "Maybe one of the restaurants I applied to called me," he said as he keyed in his message code.

Lula went to the kitchen for some water. When she returned to living room area, she noticed the stricken, upset look on Jeff's face. "Bad news?" she asked.

"Really bad," he replied.

"You're scaring me," Lula said. "You make it sound like the girl from *The Ring* left you a message."

"Worse," Jeff said ominously. "It's Great-grandma Terrio!"

"Why is that so terrible?" she asked. She'd known Jeff since elementary school and she'd never even heard of Great-grandma Terrio.

"She's an American but she married an Italian guy after my great-grandfather died. They went to live in Rome, but then he died about a year ago, and now she's back, I guess," he explained. "And she wants to come here. What am I going to do?"

"Just invite her here," Lula suggested.

"I don't think she'd understand about us living together. She's pretty old-fashioned. And this is the thing I really don't want her to know—she has no idea I'm gay. So she'll either be upset if she thinks I'm straight and we live together, or she'll be even more upset that I'm gay."

"If you don't want her to know, don't tell her."

"She'll figure it out!" he insisted. "She's sharp as a tack. What if she figures it out and drops dead of shock? It could happen. She's real old. I don't want that on my conscience—that I killed my own great-grandma with my gayness."

"Don't panic," Lula said. "We'll think of something." They stood a moment, both thinking. Then Lula began to swivel her hips and smile seductively at Jeff. "We won't tell her I live here and I could . . . ," she said in a sultry voice as she moved toward him, "show you how to act like a straight man."

Jeff's eyes went wide with panic.

"Psych!" Lula shouted. "I got you good!"

Jeff relaxed, but only a little. Then he suddenly smiled. "Wait! You might have a good idea here. Would you be willing to act as my girlfriend—just to fool Great-grandma Terrio?"

"Sure," Lula agreed. "I even have a copy of our prom picture in my wallet. It would be totally believable."

"It would!" Jeff agreed excitedly. "Now all we have to do is fix you up!"

"Me?!" Lula cried. "What do you have to fix about me?"

Jeff studied her with a critical eye. "Uh . . . ," he began hesitantly. "Maybe just a few things."

Eight

Jeff phoned Great-grandma Terrio the next morning and made up a story about having his apartment painted. Lula laughed silently as she listened to Jeff lower his voice and try to sound as macho as possible. His great-grandmother then invited him to come to the hotel room where she was staying that night. "Is it all right if I bring my *girlfriend*?" Jeff asked in his stiff imitation of a manly voice.

"Is that what you think straight men are like?" Lula asked him after he hung up. "You were acting like a deep-voiced robot."

"Hey, lay off, huh?" he said. "I was doing my best. Now we have to work on you."

Lula frowned. "Oh, yes. Tell me again. What's wrong with me?"

"Nothing is *wrong* with you," he replied. "It's just that you dress in what's comfortable instead of what's feminine."

"That's a bad thing?" Lula inquired, confused.

"You have to realize that Great-grandma Terrio is from another generation—a lot of other generations. I mean, she goes *way* back. Way, way, *waaay* back."

"I get the idea," Lula said. "She predates the Stone Age. She makes Mick Jagger look young."

"Exactly," he agreed. "So we want to make you into the kind of nice, feminine, conservative girl that Great-grandma will approve of."

"This should be a load of laughs," Lula scoffed sarcastically.

"Ah, come on," he pleaded. "Pretend we're in a play. I'll play the part of a straight guy, and you can be the little missus. Or the little miss, I guess. We'll tell her we're engaged."

"Oh, okay," she gave in. "I have to get ready for work." She patted him on the back. "And it's your first day in the kitchen! Which reminds me—I bought you a present." She ran to the refrigerator and pulled out a jar filled with green stuff that looked a little like hot dog relish. "*Recaito!* This is jarred, not frozen. It's your magic, all-purpose Cuban ingredient."

"Thanks," he said glumly.

"What a disaster!" Jeff cried as he and Lula climbed the back stairs from CeCe's Cuban Café to their apartment late that afternoon. "I forgot to defrost the meat! I burned the rice! I blackened the plantains."

"It was just your first day. You'll get the hang of things," she said. "Be happy Paulo wasn't working today."

"The crabby gay guy?"

"Yeah, but I'm still not convinced he's gay. If you mess up, he won't be as understanding as I am."

Marc met them in the hall. He had a large suitcase with him. "Ready for your makeover?" he asked Lula. "I brought some dresses and makeup and hair stuff from the theater."

"Since Marc knows about costumes and theater makeup and all, I asked him to come help sort of . . . you know," Jeff tried to explain.

"What?" Lula asked. "Are you going to turn me into an icon of young conservative womanhood?"

"Something like that," Marc concurred. "Think of it as *Queer Eye for the Female Young Republican*."

"Whatever," Lula said, unlocking her apartment door. She showered, and then sat patiently as Marc applied makeup. "Are you sure about this blue eye shadow?" she asked uncertainly.

"It's what we use in the theater, so it's all I have," Marc admitted. "Do you have something you'd rather use?"

"No," she replied. "I don't usually wear eye makeup."

"You have great long lashes, so you don't really need mascara," he said, brushing it on, anyway. "But it can't hurt."

Next, he studied her hair. "I don't know what to do," he said.

"A bun," Jeff suggested. "Great-grandma will think that's classic."

"Okay," Marc said, pulling Lula's hair back. "That's easy."

Once Lula's hair and makeup were complete, Marc handed her an outfit to try on, a pink suit with a ruffled front white blouse. She wrinkled her nose as she looked it over. "Are you sure about this?" she questioned.

"Jeff told me he wanted something conservative. This was the costume worn by the principal in our production of *Grease*," Marc explained. "The actor who wore it looked great. It's sort of classic Chanel look. It appears to be popular again this year—although this isn't exactly what they're wearing."

"If you say so," Lula said. She went to her room to put it on and then came out to check her image in the apartment's only mirror, the full-length one that hung on the bathroom door.

Her hair was gathered on top of her head in a loose bun, thick mascara was clumped on her eyelashes, and her lips were bright pink. The skirt of the suit was too large and hung past her calves.

"Give the poor girl a break!" cried Daisy, who had come in the unlocked front door.

"Too theatrical maybe?" Marc asked.

"She looks like the lead in an all-female remake of *Revenge of the Nerds*! What have you done to her?"

After hearing what they were trying to accomplish, Daisy took Lula by the arm. "I'll do your hair and makeup," she offered. "My stuff won't fit you, but a mate of mine from England left one of her suitcases behind when she visited last. While she was here, she met a biker at a club and ran off on his Harley with him. She didn't feel like carrying the suitcase with her. She was about your size."

They went to Daisy's apartment, and Lula showered again, washing away all the makeup and pulling down the bun. This time Daisy blew Lula's hair into soft waves and applied just the right amount of makeup.

They went through the friend's suitcase and pulled out a form-hugging white dress, with spaghetti straps and a hem that fell just above Lula's knees. "Amazing! It's a perfect fit!" Daisy said. "It's a shame you have to put your glasses on."

"I'm getting used to my contacts," Lula

told her. "It's easier to wear them to work. My glasses kept sliding down my nose because I was always bending over."

When Daisy and Lula returned to the apartment, Jeff was dressed in a beige suit Marc had lent him. "You look amazing," Lula told him.

Jeff didn't reply. Neither did Marc. They just stood staring at her with their mouths open. "Are you the same person who left here a little while ago?" Marc finally asked after a few more speechless moments.

"She looks bloody gorgeous, doesn't she?" Daisy said.

"My great-grandmother will never believe this," Jeff said. "Even if I were straight, why would a knock-out like Lula go out with a dweeb like me?"

Conflicting emotions whirled inside Lula. All through high school she'd avoided the makeup-and-hair fixations of most of her friends. She didn't want to trade on that. It was all so unimportant, really.

But it was surprisingly pleasant to be told she was gorgeous—to know that she could be, if she chose to. "We'd better get going," she said to Jeff.

Jeff headed for the door, but stopped to take out his earring. "I don't think Great-grandma could cope with my wearing an earring," he explained.

"Is she really that old-fashioned?" Lula asked.

Jeff stared at her pointedly. "I told you, she's really, really oooooolllld!"

Great-grandma Terrio was staying at the Paradise Beach Hotel, right on Ocean Drive. It turned out to be the same large white hotel with the vivid blue canopies where Lula had waited for Jeff on her first day in South Beach.

They phoned her from the lobby, and she told them she would come down. After a ten-minute wait, the elevator door opened and a small woman supported by a cane emerged.

Jeff hadn't been kidding. She had to be the oldest person Lula had ever seen. She wore a black dress, and her white hair was pulled back in a severe bun. Small dark eyes sparkled alertly in her wrinkled face.

"Great-grandma!" Jeff greeted her with a hug.

"My Jeffie!" she cried warmly, but then her expression slowly became suspicious, as if, upon closer inspection, she'd suspected that he was an imposter and not her Jeffie at all. Her dark eyes narrowed as she looked him up and down.

Jeff turned to Lula. "I'd like you to meet my fiancée, Lucille Cruz," he said, introducing Lula to his great-grandmother.

"Please call me Lula—everyone does," Lula said. "I'm pleased to meet you." She extended her hand to shake, but the old woman didn't take it. Instead, she turned the scrutiny she'd been reserving for Jeff onto Lula.

"You two are a little too young to be getting married, if you ask me," she snapped peevishly.

"It's going to be a very long engagement," Jeff answered quickly. "We'll probably wait years—years and years."

"That's stupid!" Great-grandma Terrio remarked. "Why wait? There are lots of women in the world. Why tie yourself to one if you're not going to marry her right away?"

"But I thought you said we were too young," Jeff reminded her.

"That's why it's stupid to be engaged," she shot back. "I'm starving. I made reservations in the restaurant here."

They followed her toward the hotel's elegant restaurant. "Your mother tells me you want to work in a restaurant," she said to Jeff.

"Yes, my hope is to become a chef someday," Jeff told her. "I'd like to go to culinary school, but until I can earn the tuition for that, I'm working in a really excellent restaurant here in—"

"Cooking is woman's work!" she interrupted him.

"Well, Great-grandma, many men have been great chefs," Jeff dared to disagree. "In fact, women have been struggling to break in as chefs and it's only been in the last twenty years that they've even been able to—"

"Cooking is woman's work!" his great-grandmother interrupted a second time.

The hostess at the restaurant led them to their table. As they entered, Lula and Jeff exchanged glances. Lula rolled her eyes. It was going to be a long evening.

"So, why are you in Miami?" Jeff asked as they ate their food.

"My dear friend Mrs. Ethel Mudge is the president of a group called Literary Women of Miami," she explained. "Mrs. Mudge has invited me to a luncheon next Thursday. It's in honor of some poet of some sort. I think she wants to entice me to join. That way, I can make a generous donation to her group."

"Lula is a poet," Jeff said.

"I never cared much for poetry," Great-grandma Terrio grumbled as she unfolded her napkin.

By the time dessert arrived, Lula shoveled through her chocolate layer cake at record speed. She couldn't wait to escape from Great-grandma Terrio. Jeff, though, was taking his time, seeming to actually enjoy the cranky old woman's judgmental statements and suspicious stares. If she heard him say, "Good point, Great-grandma," one more time, she was going to scream.

Finally, they walked her back to her room. "Thanks for dinner, Great-grandma," Jeff said as the old woman unlocked her door. "I'm sorry we couldn't have you to our place, but the paint smell is very bad."

"Our place?" she questioned.

"Jeff's and mine," Lula explained.

"You two live together?" Great-grandma Terrio asked.

"No!" Jeff said.

"Yes," Lula replied at the same time.

They stared at each other with panicked eyes. "Well, yes," Jeff said, "in a way."

"No, no, I misspoke," Lula said.

Once again, their words overlapped—each contradicting the other's.

"I think what we're trying to say is that . . . in our hearts, we *feel* as if we live together," Lula said, scrambling to recover. "But, of course, it wouldn't be right to live together until we were married."

"Yes. Legally married," Jeff agreed.

Great-grandma Terrio *harrumphed,* her black eyes boring into the two of them. But then she grabbed Jeff into a hug. "Good night, my little Jeffy. Remember to make me proud."

"Good night, Great-grandma," Jeff said, wriggling out of her tight hold.

"Night. Thanks," Lula murmured. When the woman closed the door, Lula fell backward, trusting Jeff to catch her, which he did. "Well, that was completely exhausting," she remarked.

"I know," he agreed. "Thanks for going through the torture with me."

They left the Paradise Beach Hotel and strolled down Ocean Drive, too tired out from the evening to talk. Jeff took Lula's hand, and she realized it was so comforting to walk along with her best friend. She also noticed that people were looking at them. "All dressed up, we look pretty good," she commented.

"*You* look spectacular," Jeff said.

They were passing La Bamba when the front door was suddenly opened. Enrique Reyes stepped out, blocking their path. "Sorry, excuse me," he said, stepping back into the doorway. He looked her up and down, his expression surprised but impressed.

"Looking lovely tonight," he said in a low voice, just loud enough for her to hear him. Involuntarily her lips curved into a smile, and he smiled back.

She could feel his eyes on her as she and Jeff continued on down Ocean Drive. A desperate urge to run back to him surged through her. She imagined that warm, sexy voice whispering in her ear, telling her again how lovely she looked, how much he wanted her. It caused her skin to prickle with longing.

No doubt it was how all women felt about him. He was probably only flirting with her because he couldn't tell if she was interested. She was a challenge to his title as Sex God of South Beach.

Would he still flirt if he knew how very, very interested she really was? Maybe not. With that thought in her head, she used all the self-control she could muster to force herself not to look back at him.

Nine

When Lula wandered sleepily into the living room the next morning, she flopped down on the couch and picked up the book of poetry she'd found in a book shop called Utopia Books: *Doing the Shang-a-lang on Hip-Hop Street: Poems of Nzoake Jones.* She was eager to start reading, but her stomach growled at her for not feeding it.

Still scanning the book's cover, she headed for the refrigerator. On the way, she glanced up and noticed a note that Jeff had left for her on the table.

CECE CARACAS IS AN INSANE WOMAN! SHE CAME TO THE DOOR

EARLY THIS MORNING AND TOLD
ME TO HAVE A MENU PLANNED
FOR LUNCH TODAY. COME DOWN AS
SOON AS YOU CAN. I NEED
HEEEEELLLPPPP!!!!!!

Lula forgot about breakfast and the book as she threw on clothing and ran down the stairs, tying on her apron as she went. She found Jeff in the kitchen watching a cooking show on an old thirteen-inch set. "I found the TV in that closet, behind the mops," he answered her unasked question, his eyes glued to the screen.

The cook on the channel was making a chicken potpie. "I'm taking your advice," he told her. "I'm going to make this chicken potpie recipe—but with beans, peppers, and *recaito*. How do you say 'pie' in Spanish?"

"*Pastel*," she told him.

"I'll call it 'Pastel de pollo a la CeCe's'!"

"Sounds good," Lula said. "This is going to work out fine." She ran out to the restaurant to help Paulo set up.

"You've met the new chef?" Paulo asked when he saw her.

"Oh, yes. He seems terrific!" she answered. "I worked with him yesterday and he was very good."

"Is that why he's taking a crash course in cooking from The Food Network?"

"No . . . no . . . I think he's just very . . . uh . . . cutting edge," she said. "You know, he wants to be on top of the latest trends."

Jeff brought the menu board out with the day's offerings written on it. "Very impressive," Lula commented as she read:

CUBAN SANDWICH (ROAST PORK, EL JAMÓN
CON QUESO)
FERDINAND'S FISH SOUP
LOS ESPAGUETIS Y ALBÓNDIGAS (SPAGHETTI
AND MEATBALLS)
PASTEL DE POLLO A LA CECE'S (CHICKEN
POTPIE)

"Who's Ferdinand?" she asked.

Jeff shrugged. "When I was a kid I had a picture book about a Spanish bull named Ferdinand. He was supposed to be fierce, but he really just liked flowers. He was sort of a role model for me, so I named a fish soup after him. It's Campbell's clam chowder, a can of clams, beans, and *sofrito*."

"You're a genius," Lula commended him with a chuckle.

"Yes," Paulo said sarcastically, "The *albóndigas* are an especially brilliant ethnic touch."

"There's a problem?" Jeff asked.

"Spaghetti and meatballs are not typically associated with Cuba," Paulo replied with a quick snicker of laughter.

Jeff grabbed chalk from the bottom of the board and added the words *"a la Cubana"* to the spaghetti selection. "Happy now?" he asked Paulo.

"Ecstatic," he replied in that dry, superior tone he always used. After sighing and rolling his eyes skyward, he began putting out the bottles of hot sauce.

Jeff took one of the small bottles off the table. "I'll add this to the spaghetti sauce to give it that Cuban something-ness."

"Go light with that stuff. It's red hot," Lula warned.

Jeff spun and held the bottle up in a triumphant manner. "I will torch my cuisine with the spicy flame of Cuban daring," he said dramatically and danced into the kitchen.

"I'm not kidding," Lula called after him. "You're playing with fire!"

CeCe hurried excitedly into the restaurant from outside. "Listen to me! I have great news. I was out on Ocean Drive and I saw a tour bus pull up. I got onto the parked bus and talked the driver into bringing the tourists here for lunch. We're going to have a big crowd! They're coming any minute!"

Lula followed CeCe into the kitchen. "I hope you're ready for a busy lunch crowd," she told Jeff.

A flicker of panic crossed Jeff's face, but he quickly replaced it with a confident smile. "Not to worry," he told her. He shook his hot sauce over the bowl of chopped meat in front of him. "Lula, you can make meatballs, can't you?" he asked.

"I have to wait on the people," she protested.

He grabbed her arm and pulled her in front of the bowl. "They're not here yet.

Start rolling! I have to roll out my pie crusts."

"I saw frozen crusts in the walk-in freezer," she told him. He pulled it open, went in, and reemerged with a stack of frozen pie crusts. "I'll just stick them in the microwave to defrost them," he said.

Suddenly a rumble of voices filled the restaurant. Lula threw the last meatball on a tray. "I have to get out there," she told Jeff.

The restaurant was packed with elderly people on vacation. CeCe had thrown on an apron and came out to greet them. "This group is from a retirement home," she informed Lula, taking her aside. "I'll help Jeff in the kitchen. Take their drink orders before the food."

Lula nodded and approached the first table to be seated. She started taking down orders at one end of the room until she met Paulo in the middle.

While writing down an order, she slowly became aware of a terrible smell, like burning rubber. Clutching her order pad, she hurried into the kitchen.

There appeared to be a small lightning storm going on inside the microwave. It sparked and crackled! "Oh, no!" she cried.

"Jeff, did you put metal inside there?" CeCe cried, pulling the fire extinguisher off the wall.

"I don't think so," he replied as he pulled the microwave's thick black cord from the outlet. Then his eyes widened with a realization. "The pie crusts! I assumed they were in plastic containers."

"No! They come in aluminum tins," CeCe cried.

He punched a button, and the door opened. CeCe blasted it with the fire extinguisher. "Go tell the customers everything's fine," she instructed Lula.

Lula rushed back outside. "Is something burning?" a small woman with blue hair asked.

Lula forced herself to smile. "Yes, indeed something is. The chef is preparing his flaming meatballs right now!"

"Sounds yummy!" said a man in a black wig. "Let's have some. We're starving!"

"I'll see if they're ready," she said.

Back in the kitchen, CeCe was already frying the meatballs Lula had rolled into balls. "Bring these out for a free appetizer," she told Lula and Paulo. "Jeff, how are those chicken potpies coming?"

Jeff had thrown away the top crusts, which were scorched, and was peeling the rest of the pie dough out of the burnt tins. "I can use most of this dough. I'll make little dough envelopes. I worked with a chef in New York who showed me how to fold them."

Lula and Paulo served a plate of meatballs to each table. "Compliments of CeCe," Lula told the customers.

"Are these the famous flaming meatballs?" a woman asked enthusiastically.

"Yes! They're our specialty," Lula answered. "Enjoy!"

She ran back to the kitchen for more meatballs, but had to wait for CeCe to finish frying them. "Lula, turn on the oven for me, please?" Jeff requested as he opened cans of mushroom soup along with cans of beans into the little dough pouches he'd created.

"Oh, my god!" a customer shouted from the restaurant. Lula and Paulo ran to the kitchen door to see what was wrong. A thin woman with peach-colored hair stood, clutching her throat. Her face was bright red. "Water!" she gasped. "I need water!"

Lula ran to the kitchen to fill a glass for the woman.

"Water here, too!" yelled a man. "What's in these meatballs?"

Lula saw that more than half the customers were red-faced and sputtering. It was pretty obvious that Jeff hadn't listened to her warning about the hot sauce! Paulo rushed past her, carrying a pitcher of water in each hand. She began filling glasses of water as fast as she could.

One very old man with a bald head sat contentedly downing them. Looking back quickly, Lula realized it was Mr. Smedlinsky.

"Very good spicy meatball!" Mr. Smedlinsky called out, punctuating his compliment with a booming burp. But most of the people were upset and angry that the meatballs were so hot.

CeCe hurried out from the kitchen. "I apologize for the excess heat," she told the customers. "Our chef is just over from Cuba, where everything is hot, hot, hot!"

"¡Olé!" cried Mr. Smedlinsky as he continued devouring the spicy meatballs.

"To make it up to you, lunch is on the house," CeCe added. "Allow me to recommend the potpie a la CeCe's. It's our chef's newest creation, and he assures me it's *not* spicy."

Enthusiastic murmurs spread throughout the restaurant. The outrage over the meatballs soon died down. Customers sipped their water as Lula and Paulo took their orders. Most of them took CeCe's recommendation and ordered the potpie.

From the corner of her eye, Lula noticed Mr. Smedlinsky moving among the tables, giving the elderly customers his business card. Normally CeCe didn't allow anyone to come into the restaurant to sell things. But Lula figured that because he lived in the building, Mr. Smedlinsky was sort of like a family member—a nutty family member, perhaps; but she figured there was usually at least one in every family.

Lula went back to the kitchen to pick up her order and found Jeff taking the first batch of potpies out of the oven. "They look great," she said.

"Thanks," he said as he slid one onto a plate with a spatula. Stacking her tray high, she delivered the potpies and came back to pick up more.

Soon, all the customers were served. Lula walked back to the kitchen, where CeCe and Jeff were opening large cans of fruit salad as a dessert offering. She noticed open boxes of Ritz crackers on the counter. "What did you use these for?" she asked.

"It turned out that we didn't have any unfrozen chicken to put in the chicken pot-pie," Jeff explained. "And the microwave was busted, so I couldn't defrost any. I remembered that my aunt Marie sometimes made her famous Mock Apple Pie. Instead of apples, she used Ritz crackers. She said she got the recipe from the back of the cracker box."

CeCe suddenly stopped opening her can. "Do you mean you put Ritz crackers in the chicken potpies instead of chicken."

Jeff shifted uneasily from foot to foot. "Um . . . yeah."

Paulo came into the kitchen. "You should come in here, CeCe," he said.

A low murmur was coming from the restaurant. "Oh, my god!" It was the voice of the same peach-haired woman who'd received the first too-spicy meatball.

All of them hurried out to the restaurant. The crowd was standing and clapping along as Mr. Smedlinsky bounced up and down while kicking his spindly legs out, doing some kind of traditional Russian dance. They seemed to love him!

When the music stopped, everyone applauded, including Lula, Jeff, CeCe, and Paulo.

"Look, everyone," a woman shouted. "It's the new chef who just escaped from Communist Cuba!"

"*Sí, sí,*" Jeff told them, faking a Spanish accent. "I just flew in from Havana—and boy, are my arms killing me."

Lula groaned at the bad joke, but the customers laughed and cheered.

"Oh, my god!" the peach-haired woman cried yet again. "The chicken potpie a la CeCe's is out of this world! Compliments to the chef! *¡Muy bien!*"

Jeff bent low and took his bow. Lula clapped along with the others. Who would have thought Ritz cracker potpie would be such a hit?

Ten

In the next week, Jeff's kitchen skills improved daily. Lula liked to think she was becoming a pretty good waitress, too. Her proof was that Paulo was now nodding cordially to her when she came in instead of fixing her with the deep scowl that he used to reserve for her appearances. The tips she received had grown larger, too, although there were still not many customers.

She noticed CeCe hadn't asked them for the first month's rent, which they still owed her. It was good to have a landlady who at least understood why they were so broke.

Lula had come into the restaurant for

the dinner shift and stopped just inside the front door to pick up a paper someone had slipped under it.

LOCAL RESTAURANT OWNERS!
THE NEW "BEST OF" NETWORK
WANTS TO FILM
YOUR HOUSE BAND

She continued reading on her way into the kitchen.

"What ya got there?" Jeff asked as he chopped a bunch of cilantro at the counter. He'd found a recipe and was attempting to make his own *sofrito* and *recaito*.

"See for yourself," she said, handing him the paper. The flyer announced that a new cable network called The "Best Of" Network was planning a TV show called *The Best of South Beach.* It would feature a segment that showcased the five best South Beach bands.

"Too bad this place doesn't have a band," Jeff commented, reading over the flyer. "The restaurant sponsoring the band wins a kitchen makeover."

He looked around at the kitchen with

its old, avocado green stove and refrigerators. Its glass refrigerator cases had cracks that were patched with duct tape. There was a new scorch mark on the wall where the microwave had once been. "CeCe could sure use *that* prize," he remarked.

Lula nodded in agreement. "But CeCe couldn't afford musicians," she pointed out, "and who would want to play here, anyway?"

"Why not?" Jeff asked.

"Most people who play music like to have an audience," she replied.

"Mr. Smedlinsky has been here the last two nights," he reminded her.

Lula chuckled. "Yeah, I know. He loves your spicy meatballs. But a restaurant needs more than one customer."

"Marc, Jon, and Ethan eat here a lot," Jeff said.

"That's because CeCe never charges them for anything but their sodas," Lula mentioned. "She doesn't charge us, either, which is the only reason we're able to eat. I haven't made more than twenty dollars in tips in days."

"It's great working here, though, isn't

it?" Jeff insisted. His applause from the retirement-home tourists had seemed to fill him with a new enthusiasm for his future as a chef. He now watched cooking shows continually. He was more determined than ever to become a chef. The experience had also made him fiercely loyal to CeCe's Cuban Café. He thought of it as their place.

"It's great that CeCe lets you run the kitchen, and CeCe's really the best," Lula agreed. "But we need customers. If there were more people in here, she could afford to pay you more and I'd make some decent tips."

"Ah, come on," he coaxed. "If you had a lot of customers you couldn't write your poetry all evening long." It was true. Her shifts were so slow that she'd been bringing her silver notebook with her. She'd sit at a corner table and work on her poems.

If she tired of writing, she'd read the poems in *Doing the Shang-a-lang on Hip-Hop Street*. Although she'd taken her time reading every poem over and over, she was nearly finished.

Jeff switched on the TV. His favorite

cooking show was about to come on. "Could you check the weather?" Lula requested. "Daisy and I plan to go to the Parrot Jungle, but we want to pick a good day."

Jeff began clicking through the channels. "I didn't know you wanted to go to the Parrot Jungle," he said, with an edge of sulkiness in his voice. "I would have gone with you."

"I thought you'd be glad that I'm doing something without you," Lula said carefully. "Remember you said that I hide behind you?"

"I know," he admitted. "I did say that. Okay. I'm glad Daisy and you are getting to be friends." Lula didn't think he sounded all that happy, but she didn't get the chance to ask him about it, because something on the TV had caught her eye as Jeff clicked past it.

"Go back one channel. Go back!" It was her mother! And she was holding a can of Funk-Off! "Spray away foot fungus with Funk-Off!" she chirped perkily to the TV audience. She squirted the air and inhaled the mist as if it were expensive perfume.

Lula clapped. "Way to go, Mom!" Seeing her mother made her just a touch lonely for home. She'd received several voice messages from her on her cell. She always seemed to call while Lula was working, and Lula never was able to reach her back. But it sounded like everything was going well. She'd booked another Funk-Off commercial in Toronto.

Jeff clicked again and found a station with weather for her. It would be hot with occasional showers for the rest of the week.

Out in the restaurant, Paulo sat reading a magazine called *Latin Percussion.* "Another fast-paced night at CeCe's Cuban," he greeted Lula.

"What are you reading?" he asked.

"An article on the history of the conga drum," he said.

"Do you play congas?" she asked.

"Uh-huh," he said. "My father and my grandfather did too. They taught me."

"Wow!" Lula said. She was impressed, but also surprised. Paulo didn't seem like the conga type.

She had really only ever heard congas played in the summer, when men in her neighborhood sat in the playground below her apartment and beat out rhythms that made everyone who heard them start to dance, even if was only to do a quick cha-cha or sway their hips. On steamy summer nights, when she opened her bedroom window, she'd lain in bed and listened to their playing until she fell asleep.

The men in the park had seemed kind of wild—at least when they were playing. One of them was covered in tattoos, which he showed off by wearing a skinny T-shirt.

She went to the shelf where she'd stashed her bag and took out her notebook. She opened it to the poem she'd written about Enrique.

Electric Storm
By Lula Cruz

Zap. Flash.
Quicksilver electric connection.
I have never seen
Anything like you.
Heart smash. Mind crash.
Flowing in your direction.

I have never felt
Anything like you.

His voice played in her head. *Looking lovely tonight. Lovely tonight.* Ever since he'd said those words, they'd stuck in her brain like a song that played over and over.

God! The way he'd looked at her when he'd said that! It sent a delicious shiver up the back of her neck every time she thought about it—and she thought about it constantly.

She began to write, adding on to the poem:

Your voice caresses me
Like the sexy songs you sing.
Your words snake through my
brain,
Coiling there, where they
Spark and sting!
Spark and sting!

She shut the book quickly. She didn't want to think about him all the time like this—and yet she loved to think about him, all the time.

A thumping drew her attention. As he

perused his magazine, Paulo had begun hitting the table in time with some rhythm he was hearing in his head.

She remembered a song that Gloria Estefan sang that mentioned the conga. Her mother loved it and played the song often. How did it go? *Come on, shake your body baby, do the conga. I know you can't control yourself any longer.*

She closed her eyes and listened to Paulo's tapping. It carried her back to those sweaty summer nights, lying in the dark, listening to the drums.

Opening her book again, she wrote the words that came to her.

Noche Loca
By Lula Cruz

Bang! Bang! Bang!
Going faster! Faster!
Soaring up through the summer night.
Bang! Bang! Bang!
Now the moon is throbbing!
Circled with sound.
Feeling so right.

Paulo kept drumming the table, and she continued writing to the beat. Totally involved in her words, she only half noticed CeCe come in with a tray of newly washed glasses.

As CeCe stood, putting the glasses on a shelf, she began to sway to the rhythm Paulo was pounding. She suddenly closed her eyes and began to belt out a song, singing in Spanish. *"Ay, no hay que llorar, que la vida es un carnaval y es más bello vivir cantando."*

Paulo and Lula both looked up at her. *"La vida es un carnaval!"* Paulo called out, recognizing the song.

CeCe shot him a thumbs-up and a dazzling smile as she kept on singing.

Lula was stunned! What a voice! Who knew?

Paulo banged the table, really loudly now, and CeCe sang with increased passion. She moved around the restaurant, rocking in a kind of mambo step as she sang.

Jeff came out of the kitchen to hear. He and Lula exchanged looks of shocked delight. This was amazing! Paulo actually seemed to be *enjoying* himself and smiling, for once! CeCe belted out a long, wailing note and winked at the astonished Jeff and Lula.

Jeff joined Lula at her table and laid the pink flyer down on top of her notebook, tapping it. She gazed up at him, understanding what he meant.

Maybe they *did* have what it took to make The "Best Of" Network's South Beach show. They sure couldn't imagine any music better than this!

"CeCe, are you a professional singer?" Lula asked when the woman had finished her song.

"I was, a long time ago, back in Cuba," she answered. "I was young and hot then. I sang in all the clubs. But, in nineteen fifty-nine, I came to Miami because Fidel Castro had come to power and my family was very anti-Communist. My father just showed up at the club where I was singing one night and said, 'Get your purse. We're leaving.' Once we were here in Miami, I had to help my family, so I never got my singing career reestablished."

"That bites!" Jeff cried.

"It's okay," CeCe said with a dismissive

wave of her hand. "Life is unpredictable. Besides, I'm glad to be here in America."

"How would you like to start singing again?" Lula asked her. She handed CeCe the flyer. "A musical group would bring in business. And, if you got on TV, it would be great free advertising for the restaurant. Those cable channels play the same shows over and over."

"You might even win a new kitchen," Jeff added, pointing to the part on the flyer about the prize. He turned to Paulo. "Would you be interested in drumming?"

"Possibly. My buddy, Ty, is a guitarist. He and I have been talking about getting something musical together for a while," he said.

"Would the two of you want to be paid?" CeCe asked. "I'm barely keeping the restaurant open as it is."

"Maybe if we pass the hat for tips, that would be good enough," Paulo answered. "I'll ask him."

"What would we call ourselves?" CeCe wondered.

Lula and Jeff looked at each other, clueless. Paulo shrugged.

CeCe glanced down at Lula's notebook on the table. "What's this?"

"Just a poem I'm working on," Lula answered. "I'm calling it 'Noche Loca.' 'Crazy Night.' Hey! How about that for a name?"

Paulo grinned. "I like it," he said.

"It is perfect," CeCe agreed.

Lula squeezed Jeff's arm. They were really going to start a band. And they were using one of her poem titles as their name. She immediately envisioned herself writing the back cover notes on the band's first CD. "This is so cool," she said.

CeCe nodded, thinking. "Before we start, I have something I need to ask you, Lula."

Eleven

CeCe's didn't do much business that night, as usual, but Lula and Jeff stayed there until two in the morning. They were all so excited about "Noche Loca" that the night had flown by.

Back in the apartment, Lula immediately sat at the table and began writing in her silver notebook. The question CeCe had asked her was this: Would she adapt her poem, "Noche Loca," into an original theme song for the band?

CeCe had glanced at the poem and thought it would make a great song. "It could be our signature song," she said, clearly excited at the prospect of singing in public again.

"Who would have thought I might become a songwriter?" Lula said to Jeff as she wrote. "This is so unbelievable!"

Jeff threw himself onto the couch and kicked off his sneakers. "Life is unpredictable," he said, quoting CeCe, as he punched in the message-checking code on his cell. There was one from Marc, inviting him to the opening of the play he'd just designed the costumes for, an all-male gay-themed version of *Hamlet.* The second message was from his mother, calling from New York just to see how he was. And the last one was from Great-grandma Terrio.

"Lula, I'm sorry to interrupt your creative flow," he said after listening to the message, "but I have some good news and some bad news."

Lula looked up from her writing. "Give me the good news first."

"I can arrange for you to meet Nzoake Jones."

"Shut up!" she shouted, jumping up and out of her chair so quickly that she knocked it to floor behind her. "Really? No way!"

"Way," Jeff confirmed with a smile.

Lula frowned at him, suddenly worried. "What's the bad news?"

"We'll have to go with Great-grandma Terrio. Remember Great-grandma telling us about her friend in the literary society? It turns out that it's the same group that's sponsoring Nzoake Jones's reading at Miami U. Great-grandma's friend invited her to a luncheon on a yacht in honor of Nzoake Jones, and she wants us to go with her. Would you be my pretend fiancée again?"

"I'd go as SpongeBob SquarePants if it meant I could meet Nzoake Jones," Lula told him. "She's only been my idol all through high school."

"That's a yes, then?" he teased.

"Yes, it's a yes! When?"

"Tomorrow."

"Daisy and I were planning to go to the Parrot Jungle," she remembered. "That's okay. We'll do it another time. She'll understand."

"You'll have to get all dressed up again," he warned.

"That's okay. I don't care," Lula sang out as she danced happily around the room. "I'm meeting Nzoake Jones!"

★

Although Lula was too excited to sleep until nearly four that morning, she bounced out of bed at ten to begin getting ready. She ran up to Daisy's apartment and asked to borrow one of Daisy's friend's dresses.

Daisy opened the door looking bleary-eyed, with her mascara smeared to her cheeks. "You won't mind if I pass on the Parrot Jungle today, will you?" she asked. "I'm feeling a bit dodgy. I was out all last night partying and skinny dipping at a private beach. And do you know what? It was the strangest thing—strange and a bit disturbing, really."

"What?" Lula asked.

"I think I saw Mr. Smedlinsky there dancing with some old bird—naked! Both of them! So, as you can imagine, I really didn't want to get a good look." A horrified shiver ran through her. "I'm pretty sure I heard that boom box going, though. The old geezer really gets around."

Lula laughed. Then she told her what was happening and asked to borrow another dress from the clothing trunk that

Daisy's friend had left behind when she ran off with the biker. "Absolutely!" Daisy agreed. "I'll do you up, like before."

Daisy lent Lula a form-hugging, sleeveless, flower-print summer dress with ruffles along the scooped neckline and the hem. "Look here, she even left a pair of strappy numbers to go with the dress," Daisy said, holding up a pair of sexy green high-heeled sandals.

Once again, Daisy gave Lula a full-beauty treatment, setting her hair into loose curls with hot rollers and applying makeup. "Gorgeous!" she announced when she was done.

Lula turned in front of Daisy's full-length closet mirror, pleased with the result. "Thanks," she told Daisy.

Just before noon she and Jeff went to the Paradise Beach Hotel to meet up with Great-grandma Terrio. Together they took a cab a short distance to the Miami Beach Marina. From there, a motor boat ferried them to a lavish yacht anchored out in the Atlantic.

The party was already going strong when they arrived. Stylishly dressed people in pastel shades stood chatting in small groups near a buffet table laden with elegant lunch foods. An ice sculpture carved into the shape of a flower bouquet had crab claws, caviar, and boiled shrimp nestled in its icy blooms.

Great-grandma Terrio saw her friend and went over to greet her. Lula scanned the room, searching for Nzoake Jones.

She spotted a dark-skinned woman dressed in a suit, her thick black hair, woven into many braids, cascading down her back. She was speaking to a group of women and partially turned away from Lula, but she was easy to recognize. Lula had seen the poet's picture on book jackets many times.

"There she is," Lula said, turning to Jeff. But he wasn't there. "Jeff?"

He wasn't in the room, so she went outside onto the deck. Instantly she saw him, gripping the side of the yacht and looking down into the water. "Seasick," he told her, looking distinctly pale and even slightly greenish around his cheeks.

"The boat's not even moving," she pointed out.

"Believe me, it's moving enough," he

said, and was suddenly sick over the side.

She'd always wondered why he would never ride the *Staten Island Ferry* with her. "Want some water?" she offered when he was through.

He shook his head and threw up again. "Go," he said. "Meet what's-her-name, your idol. I'll be okay. There's nothing you can do for me. If you don't mind, I'd rather be alone. I don't need an audience for this."

Reluctantly she left him there and went back inside. Once again, she found Nzoake Jones. She longed to speak to her, but the woman was always deep in conversation with one person or another. Everyone wanted to speak with her, it seemed, and Lula suddenly felt extremely unimportant and intimidated.

Music began to play at the far end of the room. Casually, Lula turned to see the band—and froze mid turn.

Enrique was on the low platform stage! His band, the Miami Hombres, were behind him.

Lula's gaze was riveted on him. He was more gorgeous than ever, his deep tan contrasting with the loose white shirt he wore over beige pants. He spotted her at the same time she saw him. Their eyes met, and she had the same sensation she'd felt the first time: an electric current running between them.

He acknowledged her with a smile and a quick wave. She returned the greeting.

He turned and said something to the band. They nodded and began to play "I Need to Know," the Marc Anthony hit. Enrique took the mike off the stand and started to sing. "They say around the way you've asked for me. There's even talk about you wanting me . . ."

Lula felt that she was in serious danger of melting into a puddle right there on the floor. He'd *told* them to play that song for her. Somehow she was certain of it. And knowing he was saying these things to her made her skin tingle with excitement.

As he sang, Enrique looked in all directions, but he kept coming back to her, holding her eyes with his own. Once, she tried to look away, but found herself drawn back to him as if pulled by a magnet.

The song ended, and Enrique jumped lightly off the low stage, leaving the band to play without him. She didn't want to seem to be waiting for him, so she hurried to the buffet and began loading her plate with food. Before she knew it, he was beside her. "What a nice surprise," he said, and then grinned. "Though maybe we shouldn't be standing so close to the food—could be dangerous."

Her heart was a jackhammer slamming into her chest, but his words made her laugh. "Good point," she admitted, stepping away from the table. God! He was gorgeous!

"You're not wearing your glasses," he observed. "Did you lose them again?"

"Contacts," she replied.

He nodded, looking her over appreciatively. "Well, you look very pretty today. Really pretty."

She didn't know whether to run away or throw herself in his arms. Caught between two opposing impulses, she stood there staring. "Thanks," she forced herself to reply after a moment.

Another awkward silence followed. Enrique broke it first. "I'm glad to see you here. I keep going back to the smoothie stand to look for you, but you're never there. Did you quit?"

Lula laughed nervously. "Oh, no. I was just filling in for a friend." She went on to tell him about CeCe's Cuban Café and how she and Jeff worked there and lived above it.

"You live with that guy I always see you with?" he asked, sounding disappointed.

"Jeff? Yeah, I live with him. . . ." She paused, giving him an inquisitive look. Then it dawned on her: He thought they were a couple! She started up quickly again. "He's gay. We're friends."

His face lit with pleasure. "No kidding?"

"Yeah. We're pals, but nothing, you know, romantic. Nothing like that," she assured him.

"Hey, that's great," he said. Lula's spirits leaped as she saw how happy this made him. She told him how she was posing as his girlfriend for the benefit of his great-grandmother.

"Do you think you should be fooling her like that?" he questioned doubtfully. "Isn't it usually better to be honest?"

"She's really old—and traditional. He doesn't want to upset her."

"I suppose," he said, though Lula thought he sounded unconvinced. "So, do you know the work of the poet who's here today?" he asked.

"She's wonderful," Lula told him enthusiastically. "I started writing poetry after I read a poem she wrote."

"Very cool. Did you get to meet her?"

"I would love to, but I don't want to bother her. I was hoping to see her read her poems, but the event is sold out."

"You should go say hi," he encouraged her. "There's no reason to be shy. She's a person. You're a person."

"I just can't," she told him.

"Have it your way, but I think you should take a chance," he said. "You might regret it later if you don't."

Now that they had started to talk, Lula found him easy to be with, direct, and interested in what she was saying. He asked what she was doing in Miami, and she told him how she planned to major in English, with a concentration in creative writing, at Miami U in the fall.

"I'm impressed," he said. "I was never much of a student. I was always more interested in music."

"The University of Miami has a music school," she told him.

"Yeah? Maybe I'll check it out. It would be helpful to get some formal training. Do they need a singer at the place you work—CeCe's?"

"Not yet, but we're going to have music soon." She told him about the competition and how they were about to start a band.

"'Noche Loca' is a cool name for a band," he said as he glanced back at his band. "I'd better go back. Do you think I could take you to dinner tonight?" He grinned, almost bashfully, yet hopefully.

"I'd love to," she replied, "but I have to work. Another time?"

"I'm singing a lot this week," he said. The sound of crashing cymbals made him turn toward the Miami Hombres. The band members were all staring at him. "I think they're mad at me," he said quickly. "I'd better go."

Lula felt almost sick. She could have

had a date with him—and she'd blown it! He hadn't even asked for her cell number! Maybe she'd insulted him by refusing to go out. She could have at least attempted to get the night off—even though there was no one else to cover for her.

She went back outside to find Jeff and saw him leaning against the side of the yacht looking miserable. "Did you meet Nzoake Jones?" he asked.

"I don't have the nerve," she admitted.

"I'd offer to go with you, but I don't think it would make a good impression if I puked all over her."

Lula smiled and brushed his hair back from his sweaty forehead. "You're right, that wouldn't be good."

"Would you hate me if I went home?" he asked.

"No," she said. "I suddenly feel like getting out of here too."

Twelve

That night Lula and Jeff reported for work in the restaurant. Jeff had napped and was mostly recovered from his seasickness, though still slightly green. "I'm better, but I'm so not in the mood to cook tonight," he said as they went down the back stairs that led into the restaurant kitchen.

"I'm not in the mood for *anything*," Lula grumbled. "I just want to lie in bed with the covers over my head." She could be having dinner with Enrique at that very moment if she hadn't acted like such an idiot.

As usual, there was no one in the restaurant in the early evening. "Don't start to prepare for dinner yet," CeCe told them when they walked into the kitchen. "I want to do something first."

She brought them into the dining area and stopped at a table where an old suitcase lay.

Paulo's friend, Ty, a good-looking Asian guy of about twenty-five, was there with his guitar. Paulo introduced them all. Lula noticed a large conga drum in a corner.

"Told you Paulo was gay," Jeff whispered to Lula. "His friend is cute."

"Maybe they're just friends," Lula whispered back.

"Yeah, sure," Jeff scoffed.

CeCe opened her suitcase and removed some wooden sticks, a copper bell, a set of maracas, and a big gourd with notches cut into it. "These are instruments I used in my act back in Cuba," she said. She picked up a stick and then the notched gourd. "This is a *güiro*. You play it like this." She ran the stick up and down the gourd's notches, producing a raspy, rhythmic sound.

"That's so cool!" Jeff cried. "Can I try?"

She handed the instrument to him, and

he began to scrape it, dancing around to the music he was creating. CeCe accompanied him by hitting together the hardwood sticks. "These are called *claves,*" she informed them. "They're great for beating out the time line of the song."

Jeff continued dancing and playing the *güiro.* "*Muy bien,*" CeCe complimented him.

"I love this. Let me play with you guys," he pleaded. "Please, please, please!"

"Who will cook?" CeCe asked.

"I'll train Marc. He told me he wants to learn so he has a skill other than theater work. Then I'll run back and forth and make sure everything is okay," he argued persuasively.

"I suppose it would be good to have another trained cook," CeCe said. "All right. I can't afford to pay him, but I can reduce the guys' rent by one third if he works the whole month. Can he start tonight, right after this rehearsal?"

Jeff took his cell phone from his pocket. "I'm calling him right now."

"Lula, would you like to join us also?" CeCe offered.

Lula shook her head and waved her hands. She loved music. She was even a pretty good dancer, but that was where her musical ability ended. Even banging a bell felt like too much of a challenge. "I'll just be the songwriter," she said.

"That is fine," CeCe told her. "How is the 'Noche Loca' song coming along?"

"It needs some more work," she admitted. "But I've added a whole other batch of lyrics and I like it so far."

"Great," CeCe said with a smile.

Paulo took the conga from the corner. He drummed along with Ty and Jeff as CeCe improvised a song, her full, rich voice filling the restaurant.

Lula watched them and wrote herself a note on a napkin: *Ask Marc, Jon, and Ethan to use their computer to submit an online application to The "Best Of" Network's band search.*

"You should have snogged him when you had the chance," Daisy remarked as she applied purple nail polish to her big toe. "*Carpe* the hot bloke! That's what I always say."

Lula chuckled. "Don't you mean *carpe diem*?"

Daisy shook her head and chuckled. "No! Forget the day! Seize the guy!"

She and Lula were sitting out on the fire escape of Lula and Jeff's apartment and discussing Lula's encounter with Enrique. Their faces were slathered in green cucumber facial mask. Daisy had set Lula's hair in rollers, and they were just finishing pedicures.

"My motto seems to be 'spoil the day,'" Lula grumbled bitterly. "How could I have turned him down? I'm hopeless, I swear! I know I'll never hear from him again."

"Don't be so easily defeated," Daisy scolded. "We'll get you all *gorg-alicious* and go sit in the audience while Enrique sings."

"Just like the twenty other females, ages sixteen to sixty, who are sitting there drooling over him every night? No thanks," she disagreed.

"I see what you mean," Daisy admitted thoughtfully. "Throwing yourself at a man is usually a successful strategy, but in this case, it could backfire. We'll have to come up with a Plan B."

Someone pounded on the apartment door. Daisy groaned and slumped against the wall of the building. "That's *got* to be Mr. Smedlinsky," she said. "He must have seen me come down here. He knows I saw him in his nuddy pants the other night, and now he thinks we're pals and I should take dance lessons from him."

"Nuddy pants?" Lula questioned.

"Nuddy, as in *nude,*" Daisy explained. She shivered, trying to shake the image from her mind. "Ever since that night, he's been really pestering me."

"I'll get rid of him," Lula said, getting up. "When he has one look at me, he'll probably run away. Gee, I hope I don't give him a heart attack."

"I'll sneak down the fire escape and go back to my apartment that way," Daisy told her.

"Don't smudge your toenails," Lula warned as Daisy began to climb down the metal ladder.

There was another knock at the door. Hobbling on the balls of her feet, Lula climbed back into the apartment and went to the door. "Mr. Smedlinsky?" she checked.

"It's me."

She opened the door and stood—facing Enrique. "Fooled ya . . . ," he said, his voice trailing off in shocked surprise.

Thirteen

After a rapid hair brushing and face scrubbing, Lula raced from the bathroom into her bedroom, glancing quickly to check that he was still there waiting on the couch. She threw off her shorts and T-shirt and pulled a denim sundress over her head. How embarrassing had that been?!

She took a deep breath to calm herself before strolling nonchalantly into the living room. "Oh, Enrique, hello. When did you get here?" she asked, as if she were seeing him for the first time.

Confusion clouded his expression. "Didn't you just let me in?"

She laughed lightly. "That must have

been *Rula,* my evil twin. She drops by now and then."

"Oh, I see," he said, smiling. "Good, because I'd much rather take you with me when I go to this." He dug two tickets from the front pocket of his jeans and handed them to her.

She drew in a sharp breath. "Two tickets to the Nzoake Jones reading!" She stamped her feet rapidly in a dance of joy. "This has been sold out forever! How did you get these?"

"I went up to her at the luncheon—after you disappeared so suddenly—and I told her that I knew a huge fan of hers. I asked if she had any extra tickets."

"And she just *gave* you these?" Of course she did. Nzoake Jones might be a great and famous poet, but she was also female. Women probably always gave him anything he asked for.

"Sorry it's such short notice," he apologized. "I'd have called, but I didn't get your number. Then I remembered that you work and live above CeCe's Cuban Café, so I looked up the address in the phone book. I hope you don't mind that I just showed up."

"It's okay! It's more than okay! It's awesome!" She threw her arms around him. Realizing what she'd done, she jumped back, blushing.

"Feel free to do that whenever the urge hits you," he assured her with a wink.

Her face had to be lobster red; she knew from the heat that it was radiating. Desperate to cover up, she yanked open the refrigerator and bent over, pretending to search through the contents. "Want something to drink?" she shouted.

He came up behind her. "No thanks— especially since there's nothing in there." It was true. The refrigerator contained only a moldy container of deli tuna and a pickle with a bite mark in it.

She turned and straightened, coming up right against his chest, their faces nearly touching. Daisy's advice about snogging him came back to her. It would be so nice. From the way he was looking at her, she didn't think he'd mind either.

But women were surely always throwing themselves at him. She didn't want to be just another one of them.

Still . . .

But, no. Probably not a smart move.

She wriggled under his arm. "We should probably go," she said, her voice unsteady, despite her attempts to sound casual.

"Hmmm, I guess so," he agreed.

Down on the street, Enrique had parked his sporty red two-seater convertible. He opened the door for her and held it. It was the first time in her life anyone had ever done that. It brought up a strange and unfamiliar feeling, as though she were someone other than herself. Not a teenager from the Lower East Side of Manhattan, but an elegant, desirable woman.

It took them less than half an hour to reach the University of Miami, in the Miami suburb of Coral Gables. When they drove in the main entrance, Lula saw the campus for the first time, other than when she'd taken the virtual video tour offered on the university's Web site. Palm trees and fountains lined the walkways that led to airy, light, mostly modern buildings. A huge lake lay at the center of the campus.

"You're going to like it here, I can tell,"

Enrique said as Lula eagerly absorbed the sights and sounds around her.

"Until today, I wasn't so sure," she admitted. "But I think you're right." They passed a sign that read, SCHOOL OF MUSIC. Lula pointed to it, recalling their conversation about the possibility of his attending college. He nodded, but looked away. It was the only time Lula had ever seen him seem ill at ease.

They arrived at the lecture hall where Nzoake Jones would be reading. People were already streaming in through the front entrance. Enrique parked, got out, and was heading over to the passenger side. Lula had been so eager to see Nzoake Jones that she'd leaped out of the car immediately. "Oh, sorry," she said, realizing too late that he had intended to open the passenger side door for her.

He smiled. "Come on. Let's go."

When the audience was seated, Nzoake Jones arrived at a lectern at the center of the hall. Before she even began to speak, Lula sensed her powerful presence and charisma. She had a majestic appearance in her flowing purple gown and African-inspired jewelry.

"'Doing the Shang-a-lang on Hip Hop Street,'" she began her poem, speaking in her strong, mellifluous voice. "'That's what we were doing the night the world split open and released its captive spirits.'"

"Wow," Enrique whispered.

"I know," Lula whispered back.

They sat there mesmerized by Nzoake Jones's every word. When the hour and a half reading ended and they got up from their seats, Enrique grabbed Lula's hand. "Let's go say hi."

He turned to go, but she stayed where she was. "I don't want to bother her."

"Come on," he insisted. "She gave us these tickets. It would be rude not to thank her."

His hand was strong and warm as he led the way down the stairs of the lecture hall. "Nzoake, you were great!" he said when he reached the poet.

Nzoake Jones hugged him warmly. "I'm so glad you could come."

He introduced Lula. "She's the huge fan I was telling you about."

Nzoake Jones shook Lula's hand. "Nice to meet you. Thank you for coming."

Lula's nervous shyness melted under the woman's warm, friendly gaze. "I am really honored to meet you," she told her idol.

"Lula writes poetry too," Enrique put in. "And you were her inspiration."

This news seemed to please Nzoake Jones immensely. "That is the best thing I've heard all day," she said.

Lula felt brave enough to mention that she was working on a poem that would be turned into a song by Noche Loca. She told her about CeCe and how she'd come from Cuba because of the Communist takeover.

After several more minutes of talking, Lula noticed that a line of people had formed behind her. "I'm hogging up all your time. Sorry," she apologized.

"It was my pleasure," Nzoake Jones said. "What a fascinating story. And CeCe's Cuban Café sounds wonderful. I hope we meet again."

Lula said good-bye, feeling completely recharged. She couldn't wait to go to school here, and to take the writing courses the university offered. "Enrique, thank you so much for bringing me here," she said when they got outside the building. She turned and stood facing him.

"I'm glad I did," he said just before he bent to kiss her.

Lula shut her eyes and melted into him as he pulled her close. His lips were warm, and she could feel his heart beating against her chest. She slid her hand around his neck and kissed him back.

Fourteen

In the next week, Noche Loca came together as a band very quickly. Paulo and Ty had played together for a long time. CeCe fell into synch with them like a professional, despite her forty-five-year hiatus. Lulu suspected she'd kept sharp by singing for herself all those years.

Jeff took to the *güiro* in a big way, wailing on the instrument as he watched The Food Network for more recipes he could adapt for his Cuban specials.

"Jeff, I like the *güiro,* but could you give it a rest for two minutes," Lula complained on the second morning, after listening to its raspy beat for an hour. "I'm trying to finish this poem, song, *thing* . . . whatever it is."

"Okay," he agreed as he took a bag from the refrigerator. "I have to go upstairs, anyway. I'm showing Marc how to make *sofrito.*"

Lula nodded and went back to writing as Jeff hurried out the door.

A moment later, he was back. "Forgot my *güiro,*" he explained, taking it off the table.

Two hours later, he returned with Marc, Jon, and Ethan. "Take a look at this!" Jeff announced, showing her a poster the size of a large book.

CECE'S CUBAN CAFÉ

PRESENTS A HOT NEW BAND

NOCHE LOCA

SIZZLING CUBAN LATIN-ROCK FUSION

Lula had just come from the shower wrapped in her terry cloth robe with her hair in a towel. "That's awesome! The colors you put behind the words are amazing"

"I found clip art of parrots and then zoomed in on the feathers using Photoshop on my computer," Marc explained.

Ethan showed her the stack of posters he held. "We printed a pile of them. Now we're going out to plaster them all over SoBe."

"You guys debut next week, so we'd better get going," Ethan prodded them.

"We're out of here," Jeff said, holding the door open for them.

The next day, Enrique picked Lula up, and they drove to the Miami Seaquarium. It was a clear, sunny day, and she enjoyed driving with the top down now that she was driving with someone—unlike Jeff—who could actually drive.

"I brought you something," he said in the Seaquarium parking lot before they got out of the car. He opened the glove compartment and took out a slim, hardcover book.

Lula took it from him. "*Finding Fossils at the Midnight Laundromat!*" she cried happily. It was the newest book of poetry by Nzoake Jones. "It just came out at midnight last night." She kissed him hard on the lips.

When the kiss ended, she reached into

the large straw tote she'd bought to replace her old canvas bag. "I have something for you, too." She handed him the exact same book.

He reached over and kissed her. Feeling bold, she licked his lower lip, biting it lightly. But then something made Lula open her eyes. Two boys of about twelve were hanging over the edge of the car, staring at them. Enrique slowly turned to face them.

The boys laughed until Enrique sprang over the side of the car and sent them screaming away. Reaching into the car, he opened the glove compartment and took out a bottle of water. Opening it, he dumped the water over his head.

"What are you doing?" Lula asked.

"It's something like a cold shower," he answered. "You get me too hot."

"Oh," she said, embarrassed yet pleased. He opened the door for her, and they headed toward the Seaquarium. They spent the rest of the day looking at the fish, dolphins, and other sea life. At around four o'clock they were watching the killer whale show when Lula suddenly remembered something. She'd promised to be back at four with a finished version of "Noche Loca" so the band could learn it in time for Saturday. "Do you mind if we leave?" she asked.

"No," he replied, getting up. "Come on. What's up?" As they hurried back to his car, she told him about the group and how she was writing a theme song for them. "I know. I saw your posters," he said.

"We're trying to get on *The Best of South Beach*," she told him.

"Yeah, I know about that competition," he said. "It will be great exposure for who-ever gets on it."

"That's what we're hoping," Lula said.

They hit heavy traffic on the way back. By the time Lula arrived at the restaurant, the rehearsal was ending. "Where have you been?" Jeff asked, sounding annoyed. "We were going to learn your song today."

"We'll learn it tomorrow," CeCe said. "The important thing is that it's finished."

"I'm sorry. I was out with Enrique and we hit traffic getting back," Lula explained.

"Enrique Reyes?" Ty asked.

Lula nodded as she tied on her apron for the evening's work. "Do you know him?"

"Not really," Ty admitted. "But a buddy of mine is in his backup band, the Miami Hombres. He says Enrique is really working them extra hard now. He's determined to get them on *The Best of South Beach*."

Why hadn't he mentioned it?

"Mr. Wonderful is in the competition?" Jeff asked her.

"I guess so," she admitted.

"Hmmm . . . ," he intoned.

"What does . . . 'hmm' . . . mean?" Lula demanded.

Jeff just shrugged.

"That is so paranoid!" she cried. "He is *not* seeing me just to get information about Noche Loca! And if you think he would do anything to hurt the band, you're wrong. He knows how important the band is to me, and he would never do that!"

"All I said was . . . hmm," he pointed out.

"Yeah, but I knew what you meant," she told him angrily.

"You said it, I didn't," he replied with a shrug.

Lula stomped off into the kitchen and picked up a tray of glasses. She couldn't remember ever being so angry at Jeff in her whole life.

Fifteen

On Saturday, CeCe closed the restaurant during the day, canceling lunch. "This is our last practice, so it has to be great," she said.

Ty, Paulo, Jeff, and Marc were rearranging tables to make a stage area in the corner of the room. "I know what we need," Marc said suddenly. "Down at the theater there's a low platform that we used as Queen Gertrude's sauna. The production is over, so we could probably borrow it."

"Hamlet's mother had a sauna?" Lula questioned, eyebrows raised.

"Believe me, this Gertrude had a *lot* of things you don't find in your traditional

Hamlet production," he told her, rolling his eyes suggestively.

"Can we get it into my van?" Ty asked. They decided they could, and hurried out to pick it up.

CeCe turned to Lula. She had the lyrics for "Noche Loca" in her hand. "I love this," she said. "Paulo, Ty, and I practiced it last night with the music that I added. We think this last stanza needs some adjustment. Something about it is different from the other verses."

Lula sat and examined the song. She compared the last stanza against the rest of the song and realized that the lines contained quite a few extra syllables. "I think I see the problem."

"Can you fix it?"

"I think so," she said, nodding.

CeCe checked her watch. "We can go over some other songs first. Can I have it revised by two o'clock?"

"That should be all right," she agreed.

She returned to her apartment and began working on the lyrics, adjusting them so they were more in line with the rest of the song. She reworked it again and again, determined to get it just right.

Her cell phone rang, and she grabbed it off the table.

"A pal of mine is lending me his Jet Ski," Enrique said. "Want to take it out with me?"

"I have to be back here by two. I have to give them the revised song I just finished." She figured she'd get back in time, run up to the apartment to grab the lyrics, and go down to the restaurant with them. If she went down now, they might want to go over it and she wouldn't be able to get away.

"Okay. We'll make it quick," he assured her. "Grab a suit and meet me by the smoothie stand."

"I'll be right there." She put on her suit and a pair of shorts, then hurried down to the smoothie stand.

"Enrique said to tell you he's getting the sea-contraption thing going. He'll be down at the water's edge," Daisy told her. "God he's gorgeous!"

"I know," Lula agreed, smiling. "You're coming to CeCe's tonight, aren't you?"

"Wouldn't miss it," she confirmed.

"The posters look smashing. They're everywhere. Have you heard back from the 'Best Of' people?"

"Not yet. Jeff's calling them," Lula replied. "Keep your fingers crossed." She waved and went down to the beach to the water's edge.

Enrique was sitting in the shallow water, just beyond the breaking surf, on a brand-new Yamaha Waverunner two-seater Jet Ski. He was the only guy she knew who could make a life preserver look hot and stylish. "Hop on," he said.

She pulled on the life preserver he handed her. "Have you ever driven one of these before?" she asked as she seated herself behind him.

"Sure. It's easy." He turned the throttle, sending the Jet Ski speeding over the waves. Lula held him tightly as the ocean spray covered her with its salty mist. Leaning her head against his strong back, she felt completely exhilarated. She couldn't imagine ever feeling more alive than she did at that moment.

He drove them far along the shoreline, down past South Pointe Park and into

Biscayne Bay. He pulled into a small beach by an outdoor restaurant. "This thing is great on gas," he commented as they climbed off. "The needle hasn't even moved off the Full mark."

"That's good," she said, giving it a casual glance. "Do we have time for this?"

He checked his watch. "We'll be back in time," he said confidently.

They sat overlooking the bay, eating lobsters that were sweet and tangy. Lula looked at his deep brown eyes with their gold and green lights and was sure Jeff had been wrong about him. But . . . still . . . she needed to know. "Are you and your band trying for *The Best of South Beach* spot?" she asked.

"Yeah," he said, dipping his lobster into melted butter.

"Why didn't you tell me?"

"Why should I tell the competition what we're doing?"

Lula was speechless. Had Jeff been right after all?

"What?" he said, noticing her stunned silence. "What's wrong with that?"

"I told *you* about Noche Loca," she said.

"I know, and since it's a new band I didn't want to get you all nervous about competing against us."

"Don't you think Noche Loca can compete against the Miami Hombres?" she challenged. "We may be new, but CeCe Caracas is an unbelievable singer."

"Listen," he said, sitting back in his seat, "they are going to pick five bands. I personally know of four bands playing right now that are so hot, you can't touch them. So that leaves one spot. I want to win it."

"So you admit it!" she cried.

"What are you talking about? CeCe's band wants to win too. So, we're in competition?" He shrugged, as if to say, *no big deal.* She didn't like it, though. The feeling that he hadn't been completely honest bothered her.

Suddenly, the lobster didn't taste as delicious. "I'd better get back," she said. "It's getting late."

Enrique paid the bill, and they got on the Jet Ski. They headed out of the bay, around the point, and back into the Atlantic. They were still far from shore when the engine began to sputter.

"What's wrong?" Lula asked as the engine coughed and suddenly died.

"I don't know," he told her. He tried it again, and it still wouldn't run. "There's a compartment behind the seat. My cell phone is in there," he told her.

He phoned someone and, while he talked, Lula checked the time on his watch. It was nearly two. She looked to the shoreline but decided she couldn't swim that far.

"My friend says he's been having trouble with the fuel line," he told her. "He's coming with his motor boat to get us."

They sat on the floating Jet Ski, not talking for almost three minutes. "Sorry," he said after a while.

She nodded, not looking at him.

"About the band," he added. "May the best band win, you know? It's a fair competition, right?"

"Right," she agreed, but she still didn't feel easy about the whole thing.

Enrique's friend didn't arrive for an hour. He drove back slowly since he was towing the Jet Ski. Lula used Enrique's phone to call Jeff, but she kept getting a message. He'd probably silenced it since they were rehearsing. She phoned the restaurant but got a busy signal.

By the time Enrique's friend got them ashore, it was nearly three thirty. "I have to go," she said to Enrique, giving him a quick kiss.

Daisy waved to her as she hurried past the smoothie stand. "Jeff was down here looking for you," she shouted. "You're supposed to bring them a new song or something."

"I know! I know!" Lula shouted back without slowing her pace.

She got to the apartment feeling sweaty and irritated. She'd been working on the new words to "Noche Loca" in her notebook, and now she ripped them out quickly. In her hurry, they fell to the floor. As she scooped them up, she saw that she'd also ripped out the love poem she'd written about Enrique. She folded that page and stuck it inside *Finding Fossils at the Midnight Laundromat,* which lay on the table.

She turned to go out again when she nearly crashed into Jeff on his way in. "Rehearsal is over," he told her. "We can't do the song tonight. Where were you?"

"I went out on a Jet Ski with Enrique, and it conked out in the middle of the ocean," she explained.

"A Jet Ski?" he cried indignantly. "It's Noche Loca's opening night—and you're zooming around on a Jet Ski with the enemy?"

"He's not the enemy!" Lula sat down at the table and stuck the lyrics in the Nzoake Jones book along with the love poem. "Jeez, you're starting to sound like your uncle."

"The guy takes you out where you can't possibly get back. He strands you there— the old engine-trouble trick. He knows you're working on a song for the group. And he just happens to be the lead singer in a band that wants the same TV spot we trying for!"

"Are you saying he planned it?" Lula asked.

"Ah, duh? You think?"

"No!" she cried. "I don't think. What I think is that you're jealous that I'm spending time with him and not you. You said I was hiding behind you, but it's the other way around. You don't want me to have a boyfriend because then you're on your own." As she spoke, tears sprang to her eyes. Angrily, she stormed into her bedroom, slamming the door behind.

She stood by the door with her hands over her face, trying to calm down. In a few minutes she heard the sound of an aerosol can being squirted and somehow she just knew what it was. He was spraying Funk-Off at her bedroom door.

Sixteen

Noche Loca debuted at ten o'clock on a Saturday night. The group started with the song CeCe had sung the very first day they'd decided to form a musical group, "¡La Vida Es un Carnaval!" Then the band moved right into the Ricky Martin hit "Livin' La Vida Loca."

By the time they'd finished "Livin' La Vida Loca," CeCe and the band had completely captured the audience. The song sounded all the more intriguing because CeCe sounded nothing like Ricky Martin; she really made it her own. They went on to perform the Shakira song "Suerte," and the Marc Anthony song "Ahora Quien."

Jeff worked the *güiro* like he'd been doing it all his life, and Ty's melodious guitar work somehow made all the pieces come together.

CeCe sang Gloria Estefan's "The Conga," and midway through it Paulo did a solo on his conga drums. CeCe's voice seemed to fill the entire room when the band finished up with the Tito Nieves hit "I Like It Like That."

After their first set, they received a standing ovation. Mr. Smedlinsky was the first to jump up, waving his fork with one of Jeff's spicy meatballs speared at the end. Then the handful of other people in the restaurant followed.

"Tell your friends," Lula said to every customer she waited on. "Tell them to come and check out the music." She handed each customer one of the posters.

She was glad Marc was working in the kitchen. She was in no mood to deal with Jeff.

"What did you think?" CeCe asked between sets.

"You were great," Lula told her sincerely.

"Thank you. And how about your friend on the *güiro*?" CeCe added.

"Okay, I guess," she said. In truth, Jeff had been pretty amazing up there, playing and moving to the beat like a professional musician. But all she could see was a mental picture of him blasting her door with Funk-Off.

The second set brought in more people, and by the last set of the night the restaurant was half full. It was the most business they'd done since Lula had been there. The late-night diners had appetizers and desserts instead of dinner, but they tended to leave the same tips as if they'd had a full dinner.

Noche Loca was finishing up at around two in the morning when she saw that Enrique had come in. She had served her last customer and was sitting at a corner table, watching the performance. "Can I sit down?" he asked.

She gestured for him to pull up a chair. She knew he'd just come from performing at La Bamba, because he was dressed less casually than usual.

"I caught the band's last number," he

said. "They really have chops. CeCe's incredible."

"I'm amazed by how great they are," Lula agreed.

He leaned forward. "Are you mad at me?"

His directness was so disarming, she couldn't be angry at him. "No," she said softly.

"Good, because I want you to come out with me tomorrow morning around ten," he said.

"Why?"

"It's a surprise. You'll see," he said. "I'll come get you."

"I have to be back by twelve so the band can learn the new words to the song."

"We'll be on dry land the whole time. We won't even drive. I promise." He kissed her lightly on the lips and left.

Lula got up to clear away the last of the dishes. When she carried a basin of them into the kitchen, CeCe was on the phone. "They're coming," she said, hanging up. "The *Best Of* people will show up in the next few days. But they won't say when. The show's host and a cameraman will just arrive unannounced."

"That's great," Lula said.

"You know, doing covers of other people's songs is fine, but a group doesn't make a name for itself that way. Lula, your words are really good," CeCe said. "If we could sing it, it would set us apart—you know, be our signature original song."

"I'll run upstairs and get the new words," Lula offered.

"Don't bother," CeCe said. "I'm too tired to look at them tonight. Just bring them at twelve, when we practice again. I'm not going to open for lunch until we have the *Best Of* tryout. I'm sorry that you won't make the lunch tips."

"It's fine," Lula said. "I made more tips tonight than ever before."

CeCe nodded and smiled. "Jeff's cooking and your idea about this band will keep this restaurant going. I owe it all to the two of you."

Enrique showed up at the apartment at 9:45. "Bring the new Nzoake Jones book I gave you," he told her. "I have mine." He held up the slim volume and tossed it down on the table beside her copy. "She's signing them at Utopia Books on Jefferson Avenue. She sent me a postcard saying that if we got there by ten or so, she'd sign ours first before the signing officially begins."

"Utopia Books is just a few blocks away," Lula remembered excitedly. "Give me a second in the bathroom and I'll be right there." In the bathroom she finished putting on some gray eye shadow and mascara. She came back out and found him leafing through the book.

"Have you read any of it yet?" she asked, picking her book up from the table.

"A few poems," he replied. "I like them. They're exciting." He grabbed her around the waist and pulled her in close. "Like I like you."

The kiss was long and passionate. Still kissing, he backed her up against the refrigerator and leaned his weight into her. "We should go," she said when they broke.

He took a deep breath. "You're right. We should."

It was just a short walk to the store that specialized in rare art books and vintage children's books. When they stepped inside, Nzoake Jones was seated at a table near the door.

"So nice to see you again," she greeted them.

They presented their books, and the poet wrote a short inscription along with her signature. To Enrique, she wrote: Thanks for the gift of your song. May you sing for the whole world someday. She inscribed Lula's book: Keep writing, poet woman. Let the words carry you higher.

"How are things going at that magical café of yours?" she asked Lula.

"Great," she replied. "It's right around here. Noche Loca is playing tonight."

"It sounds like an experience," the poet commented.

People began coming in for autographs, so they said good-bye. "You've never been to my place," Enrique said as they came out on the sidewalk. "Want to see it? It's just a block away."

There would be no twelve-year-old boys staring at them in his apartment—no one to stop them from doing . . . anything. Was she ready for that?

Her heartbeat picked up speed. "All right," she said.

Lula hurried down Española Way back toward her apartment. It was 12:45.

As she'd pretty much expected, one thing had led to another with Enrique once they'd gone to his apartment. It surprised her that Enrique hadn't pressed her to go all the way and have sex. But she was relieved, in a way. He was so hot, but she wasn't sure she was ready to take that step. Maybe it would just take more time for her to trust him completely.

And even without going all the way, it had been amazing. He was passionate, and gentle, and sexy—all at the same time. It had been so exciting that she'd completely lost track of time. And that was why she was angry with herself now. How could she be late a third time?

She burst into the apartment and tossed her signed copy of the Nzoake Jones book on the table. Where was her notebook? Maybe she could get the words to "Noche Loca" to the band while they were still rehearsing.

Turning, she saw the silver notebook on the couch. The moment she picked it up, she remembered that she'd torn out the pages containing the lyrics.

Where could she have put them?

She was in her bedroom searching through her bedroom drawers when Jeff entered the apartment. Rushing out of her room, she faced him. "I can't find the lyrics to the 'Noche Loca' song. Have you seen them?" They were the first words she'd spoken to him since their fight.

"Nope," he replied curtly.

"I was working on them in the living room. They have to be here."

"I think we're just forgetting about the song, anyway," he said coldly.

"You can't!" she cried, throwing her arms out from her side. "This is all your fault, you know."

"My fault?"

"Yes," she insisted. "I had them in my hand the other day, and then you came in attacking me with your paranoid theories about Enrique."

"Oh, yeah. I'm real paranoid," he scoffed sarcastically. "I wonder why you didn't make it to practice today."

How did he know she'd been out with Enrique? He must have seen him come into the building.

"Ty says Enrique is practicing with the Miami Hombres day and night, trying out new songs, getting really tight," Jeff went on. "And every time you're with him, he keeps you from delivering the song you're supposed to be writing. I'll bet he has those lyrics. His band will probably perform your song when the *Best of* people show up."

"You have a warped mind," she said.

"Think what you like," Jeff said, sitting on the couch to check his cell phone messages. After a moment, he got up. "Great-grandma Terrio wants us to come over tonight. I'm going to tell her you're sick."

"Go ahead," Lula shouted at the bathroom door, which he'd closed behind him. "One more lie won't make a difference, especially since you've already told her about a hundred."

She paced back and forth across the apartment, fuming with anger. "In fact, tell her that we broke up! At least that would have *some* truth to it!"

Seventeen

That night, CeCe's place was almost half full from the very first set. Jeff had taught Marc to make his famous Ritz cracker pot-pies, and Lula couldn't seem to serve them fast enough along with big, cold drinks.

Around nine thirty, Lula pulled Marc out of the kitchen and pointed to a man sitting alone at a table in the corner. "Do you know who he is?" she asked. "He's been sitting there writing for an hour."

Marc stared at him, thinking. "I've seen him before, but I don't know where." After several more minutes, he snapped his fingers, remembering. "He writes about music and theater for the *Miami Herald*.

He's not their regular writer, but he contributes an article now and then. He reviewed our *Hamlet* . . . called it 'daring but misguided.'"

Lula crossed her fingers. "I hope he likes Noche Loca."

"How could he *not* like them?" Marc asked. Before returning to the kitchen, he took a small digital camera from his pocket and snapped pictures of the band. "Isn't technology great?" he commented, slipping the camera back in his pocket.

More than ever, she wished she'd gotten the Noche Loca song to the band so they could have made a great impression on the reviewer.

It was almost ten when Nzoake Jones arrived with about eight people. Lula ran to greet her. "I'm so glad you came," she said, leading the poet to a large round table.

"I had another poetry reading and I brought some people back with me. I love Latin music," she said.

"Then you'll love this," Lula assured her.

The restaurant was three quarters full

by the last set. Many of the customers simply hadn't left after they'd finished their meals, and more people kept coming in.

"I think you'd better get the *tapas* menu ready," she advised Marc. It made Lula remember the first day they'd walked into the restaurant and CeCe had offered them *tapas,* explaining that the word meant "little dishes."

Lula waited on customers while the band went onstage. CeCe had already launched into her first song when a raucous, laughing crowd of twelve people came in. "Lulabelle!" a familiar voice cried.

Lula turned to her father and waved.

"How's it going, baby doll?" he asked, coming over to her. "Can you get us a table?"

"We can push some tables together," she said. "Could you help me?"

"Sure thing." Ruben Cruz got some of his friends to slide the tables and form one long one. "Everybody's talking about this place," he said as they worked. "They say this band is hot!"

"It is," she agreed. She brought her father's friends drinks, and they ordered small dishes from the *tapas* menu. When the band did "The Conga," her dad and his friends jumped up to form a dance line.

As they danced around the room, Nzoake Jones and her friends got up to join them. Mr. Smedlinsky grabbed on at the very end, kicking his legs out wildly as they group-danced around the restaurant. "Come on, Lulabelle!" her father shouted when the group danced by her. Lula put down the menus she was holding. She grabbed Mr. Smedlinsky around the waist and joined the others as they moved to the beat.

The group had moved toward the front door when another set of hands grabbed her waist. She turned and saw Enrique behind her. "Oh, excuse me. I thought you were Jennifer Lopez," he teased as he danced along.

She smiled at him, recalling the exciting time they'd had at his apartment that morning.

He danced very close to her. "Can you come to my place after you get off work?" he whispered in her ear.

"It might be late," she answered. "This

crowd doesn't seem to want to leave."

"It's okay," he replied. "I'll wait."

"¡Wepa!" her father shouted from the front of the line.

It was two in the morning when Lula finally wiped the last table clean. The critic had stayed until one o'clock; she wondered what he would write.

"Everything all right, Lulabelle?" her father asked before he left.

"Everything's fine," she said, not wanting to tell him all the details of her life.

He pressed a hundred-dollar bill into her hand. "You know where I am if you need anything, right?"

She nodded. "Thanks."

"I'm going to be coming around here a lot more often now that I see that you have such great music," he added. "Your friend Jeff really hits it on that *güiro*."

"You know the *güiro*?"

"Don't you remember me playing it when we had parties in the apartment?" She shook her head. She had no memory of that at all. "Well, you were just a baby, I guess," he said, kissing her on the forehead before leaving.

Lula rushed through the rest of her closing chores so she could go see Enrique. When she stepped out the front door, he was waiting, leaning against a wall of the building. "I didn't want you to walk alone," he said. "It's late."

She experienced the same rush of feeling as when he'd opened doors for her. No one had ever before pampered her, or seemed to care so much about her safety.

He put his arm around her waist, and they walked quickly to his place. They took the elevator up to the simple one-bedroom apartment.

As soon as he shut the door, they were in each other's arms, kissing passionately. He backed her against the arm of the couch and, still locked in their embrace, they toppled onto the couch. Her purse fell from her arm, and the contents clattered across the tile floor.

Both of them stopped to see what had fallen. "It's okay, leave it," Lula said.

He lifted himself off her. "Oh, that reminds me," he said, standing, "I have a gift for you."

He went into the bathroom, and she

began to pick up the items that had fallen. She found his copy of *Finding Fossils* under the couch and put it on the coffee table.

He returned from the bathroom with an annoyed expression on his face. Then his face brightened as he recalled what he'd done. "I left it in my car! It's parked just outside. Be right back." He kissed her hard on the lips and hurried out.

The phone rang right after he was gone. Lula wondered who could be calling at 2:30 in the morning.

It's Enrique. I'm not here. What's happening? The recorded message on his answering machine played.

"It's Paco, man," the voice on the other end of the phone came on. "I guess you're out spying on the competition. Or maybe you're making time with their songwriter. We could sure use that song she's writing. Call me."

Lula felt as if her heart were suddenly pumping ice water. At the same moment, she caught sight of a corner of paper peeking out of *Finding Fossils.* It was the same paper from her notebook.

Opening the book, she drew in a sharp

breath of horrified disbelief. There were her lyrics to "Noche Loca"—the missing paper she'd torn from her notebook. He must have picked it up when he was at her place.

Tears jumped to her eyes as she grabbed her purse and stuffed the paper inside.

He was standing in the doorway when she pulled the door open. She pushed past him into the hall. He followed her as she stormed to the elevator. "Lula, what's going on?"

"Don't speak to me," she said through her tears. "Ever!"

"Don't go. I'll walk you home," he said. "What happened?"

The elevator door opened, and she stepped in. He got in, too, but she shoved him back out just as the doors closed. As the elevator got lower and lower, she kicked the wall, leaving a scrape. As soon as the elevator got to the lobby, she ran out, her eyes still streaming with tears.

When she was near CeCe's, she didn't feel like going up to the apartment. Jeff might be up, and she just wanted to be alone. Instead, she kept going until she reached the beach and went on down to the water's edge. There she sat in the sand, buried her face in her hands, and cried as if she would never stop.

She was crying so hard that she wasn't aware that someone had come up beside her.

"Are you okay, Lula?" Jeff asked, crouching beside her.

She wiped away tears and blinked at him in the darkness. The moonlight illuminated his face and shoulders. "I'm not hurt or anything."

"Then what's wrong?" he asked, his voice filled with worry. "Marc and I were walking down Ocean Drive and I saw you run down here, so I followed."

"Where's Marc?" she asked, sniffing.

"I told him to go on without me," he answered. He sat down on the sand beside her. "I don't want to fight anymore," he told her. "I'm sorry for the things I said about Enrique. Maybe you're right. I guess I *was* a little jealous that you were spending so much time with him instead of with me or the band."

"Don't be sorry," Lula said. "You were

right." She told him what had happened, about the phone message and finding the lyrics tucked in his book. "I should have known a guy as hot as he is wouldn't be interested in someone like me."

"What do you mean, someone like you?" Jeff asked, putting his arm around her. "Do you mean someone beautiful, talented, and fun to be with?"

His comforting words made her start crying all over again. She laid her head on his shoulder and let the tears come. They sat there a long time with the surf crashing nearby and the moon shining on them, feeling closer than ever before.

Eventually, Jeff stood and extended his hand to Lula, pulling her up. "We'd better get some sleep," he said with a yawn. They walked across the sand back to Ocean Drive. Despite the hour, there were still people on the street.

Lula's cell phone rang in her bag. "Enrique?" Jeff suggested.

"Probably," Lula agreed, taking her phone from her bag and shutting it off.

Eighteen

"¡*Miren!* Look at this, everybody! Look at this!" CeCe ran through the restaurant holding that day's *Miami Herald.* She slapped it down on a table, opening it to the nightlife section.

Lula, Jeff, and Marc ran in from the kitchen. Paulo and Ty were already in the restaurant and ran to CeCe's side. They all gathered around to see what she was pointing to.

CECE'S CUBAN CAFÉ, NEW HOT SPOT IN TOWN

The article featured photos. One showed Noche Loca playing. CeCe was hitting a long, high note in the picture. The other featured the dance line, with Nzoake Jones looking like she was having the best time of her life. A third closed in on Jeff playing the *güiro*.

"Who took these?" Lula asked.

Marc took his compact digital camera from his pocket. "Technology is a beautiful thing," he said. "When I saw the reviewer, I thought he could use some pictures. I called my friend from the theater because I remembered she had the reviewer's e-mail address. Then I loaded the pictures and e-mailed them."

"Way to go!" Jeff cheered. He and Marc high-fived with a satisfying smack of hands.

CeCe read the article aloud. "'It was all good—great music, fun crowd, with the occasional celebrity like Nzoake Jones dropping by, and excellent service.'"

"'Excellent service,'" Lula repeated, smiling at Paulo.

"You've come a long way, baby," he commented.

"'The unique food, like the music, is an original fusion of Latin and rock 'n' roll,'" Jeff read on. He and Marc turned to each other and high-fived a second time, then turned and did a backward low five.

Over on the shelf, Lula's bag rang. "Oh, I forgot to turn that thing off," she said. She retrieved her phone and turned it off mid ring.

"Don't you care to find out who it was?" CeCe asked.

"I know who it was," Lula replied, "and no, I don't care."

Lula dug deeper into her bag and pulled out the words for "Noche Loca," the song. "I don't know if you have time to learn this, but here's the song I wrote," she told them.

"Ah, *muy bien*," CeCe cried happily. "I've written some music for it. Let's see if we can make it all fit together."

For the next two hours they worked on the song. Lula adjusted words here and there to fit the music, but CeCe's experience with songs made it all mesh. "Let's stop for a conga solo midway," she suggested. "Then, later on, Ty can play some Spanish guitar with Jeff accompanying him on the *güiro*. Sound good?"

"Sounds good," Paulo agreed.

After a lunch break for ordered-in pizza, they went back to work on the song. Each time they tried it, the effect was more dynamic. "This will cinch it for us," Jeff said, smiling at Lula. "The *Best of* people are going to be knocked out."

"When are they ever going to come?" Lula worried.

"They're around," Ty told them. "Paco told me they were at La Bamba last night."

"Paco, ugh," Lula snorted.

"You know him?" Ty asked.

"I heard his voice on an answering machine and I can't say he's my favorite person," Lula said.

Ty shrugged, deciding not to probe any further. "Anyway, they were there filming."

CeCe put a sign on the door saying that the restaurant would open at 6:30. Glancing down from her fire escape at 5:45, Lula realized that people were already waiting around on the sidewalk in front.

She climbed back into the apartment, where Daisy was working on a jigsaw puzzle that was supposed to be a handsome young black man in an extremely small bathing suit. It was a gift from her boyfriend, Albert, back in West Sussex who'd had a photo of himself made into a puzzle and sent it to her.

"Did you find Albert's rear end yet?" Lula asked.

"Not yet, but I'm having fun searching for it," Daisy replied.

"Have you ever waited tables?" Lula asked her.

"Since I was thirteen," she answered, still sorting through the puzzle pieces. "My dad owns a pub. And then I used to wait tables for CeCe when I first got here."

"Oh, right. I think you mentioned that. Would you want to do it tonight? I have a feeling I won't be able to handle the crowd we're going to get by myself."

"Okay," she agreed, "if you like."

At 6:30, CeCe opened the doors and the crowd poured in. Lula noticed that CeCe wasn't her usual smiling, robust self. "Is anything wrong?" she asked her.

CeCe rubbed her stomach. "I'm feeling a little funny," she revealed. "Some Alka-Seltzer—perhaps that will help."

She hurried off, and Lula was instantly busy seating customers and taking their orders. Jeff and Marc had made lots of Ritz cracker potpies, now also known now as CeCe's Specialty de la casa.

Noche Loca sang their first set, and the crowd was with them from the first note. Lula congratulated herself for having the foresight to ask Daisy to help. There would have been no way she could have handled this crowd alone.

Lula was bringing a tray of drinks to a table when she heard CeCe falter on a note. She looked around. No one else appeared to have noticed. But that wasn't like CeCe.

Midway through the set, a woman walked in and with her was a man with a large camera positioned on his shoulder. Lula hurried up to them. "I'm Beth Minor. We're filming this for the 'Best Of' competition," the woman told her. "Mrs. Caracas has given us permission to—"

"Absolutely," Lula said, cutting her off. She guided them down into the crowded restaurant.

"We don't need a table," Beth Minor told her. "We'll stand."

"Great," Lula said, "because it's standing-room-only. Noche Loca is the best South Beach has to offer."

The cameraman leaned against the wall. "He won't start shooting until the next set," Beth Minor told Lula. "We want to catch the whole thing from start to finish."

Lula was hurrying to her next table when she saw Great-grandma Terrio come in with her friend, Mrs. Mudge. What was she doing there? Lula hurried up them. "Hello," she greeted them.

Great-grandma Terrio frowned at her, and Lula remembered that she'd been told that Jeff and Lula had broken up. "You work here, Lula?" she asked coldly.

"Yes. Are you here to see Jeff?"

"I'm here to see CeCe Caracas. Why would I come here to see Jeff?" Great-grandma Terrio asked. "Jeff runs a marble importing business. Why would *he* be here?"

Marble importing? At least when Jeff lied, he lied big. "Well . . . uh . . . in his spare time he performs in the band here," Lula covered for him.

"My great-grandson is in a band with CeCe Caracas?" Great-grandma Terrio cried, sounding astonished yet delighted. "Let me see!" Leaning on her cane, she moved with surprising speed into the restaurant.

She got there just as the set was ending. Everyone was on their feet clapping. Marc came out of the kitchen to join the applause.

Happy and filled with exuberance, Jeff jumped off the low platform stage and hugged Marc. The two of them held each other in a tight embrace, rocking back and forth. Then Marc pulled back and kissed Jeff on the lips.

Lula stared. If she hadn't been so preoccupied by Enrique, she probably would have seen what was going on much sooner. It wasn't really that surprising—and Marc was a great guy.

Still, she experienced a pang of loss, suddenly keenly aware of how Jeff must have felt when she became involved with Enrique. She blamed herself for being insensitive. Well, it was her turn, and she figured she could deal with it.

The clapping continued. Mr. Smedlinsky stood on a chair, whistling with his fingers in his mouth.

Jeff and Marc kissed again and then did a high five. He turned around for a behind-the-back low five—and faced Great-grandma Terrio. From her stunned expression, it was clear that she'd seen him kiss Marc.

Jeff moved toward her, pale and shaken. "Great-grandma . . . ," he began.

Great Grandma Terrio held up her hand to stop him. "I saw what you did," she said with icy disgust. "You are no longer my great-grandson."

Jeff staggered back as if she'd slapped him. Then he lunged forward and ran out the front door.

Nineteen

"He's not back yet?" Daisy asked Lula as she lifted a tray of potpies onto her shoulder.

Lula shook her head. "He was completely freaked. I hope he's okay. He didn't want his great-grandmother to know he's gay."

"Do you mean she just found out tonight?" Marc asked as he took a tray of potpies from the oven.

"Yeah. That's why I was pretending to be his fiancée," Lula replied.

"I know. You were his beard," Daisy added.

"His what?" Lula asked, opening the

refrigerator case to take out cans of soda.

"His cover, his fake girlfriend," Daisy explained. "When gay men have pretend hetero mates, it's called having a beard. Movie stars do it all the time."

"How do you know?" Lula asked.

"In England we're hip to all these tricks," Daisy insisted as she went out the kitchen door. "You Americans are so naive."

Lula wondered if she *was* really naive. Enrique had certainly fooled her. Just thinking of him made her sigh, partly from missing him, despite everything; partly from the sadness of being betrayed. She felt so totally used. It would have been beyond great if he had really been the person she'd thought he was.

CeCe came in and sat heavily on a stool in the corner, her head leaning against the wall. Her skin had taken on a greenish undertone. Lula put her hand on CeCe's forehead. "You're hot, CeCe," she announced.

"Thank you," CeCe replied.

"I mean, you have a fever!"

CeCe slid off the stool, pushing herself

away from the wall. "I'll be okay. The *Best of* folks are going to film this set. Did Jeff come back?"

"Not yet?"

"What happened?" she asked.

Lula and Marc told her how Jeff was trying to conceal his gayness from his great-grandmother. CeCe stuck her head in the refrigerator case and shut her eyes, enjoying the frigid blast. "It was pretty sudden for her, I suppose."

"She doesn't know *anything* about him!" Lula cried. She was thinking about how people who were supposed to be close—to be family, even—could be so hidden from one another. Jeff's great-grandmother thought he was someone completely different from his true self. But it was true in her own life too. She'd thought she was in love with Enrique and that he loved her too. Yet she hadn't seen what a snake he was at all.

CeCe pulled her head back and closed the case. "His great-grandmother looks so familiar, but I cannot place her."

"That's interesting, because she came to see you," Lula told her, "not Jeff."

"Hmm . . . well, I cannot think about it

now," she said, hurrying to the narrow bathroom at the back of the kitchen.

Daisy came back into the kitchen to pick up another order. "They're waiting for CeCe out there," she said, loading her tray.

CeCe came out at that moment. "I am coming!" she said, walking quickly back out to the restaurant.

The restaurant was now completely packed. People stood along the back walls. Lula was pretty sure they were over the limit of people allowed by the fire code, but she was too busy to stop to count.

The *Best of* cameraman was standing. He scanned the audience with his camera. Lula looked around to see what he was seeing. Jon and Ethan sat at a table with some of their other friends. Mr. Smedlinsky was there eating the spicy meatballs that Marc and Jeff now made every night, specially for him. And, standing in a corner, was . . . Enrique.

Lula was startled when she saw him, nearly unsettling the drinks on her tray. How could he come in here? What nerve!

CeCe spoke into the microphone, even though Jeff hadn't yet returned. "Welcome to CeCe's Cuban Café," she said to the crowd. One hand suddenly flew to her mouth, and she clutched her stomach with the other. In the next second she was off the stage, rushing toward the kitchen bathroom.

Paulo went to the microphone. "Sorry, but our lead singer is too sick to perform tonight, and our *güiro* player has gone missing, too, so we'll have to cancel the performance."

A disappointed groan spread throughout the restaurant. Customers instantly began calling for their check. The *Best of* cameraman put his camera down.

Mr. Smedlinsky jumped up onto his table. "No leave! Jerzy Smedlinsky entertain for you!" He switched on the boom box on a chair at his table and began his wild version of the rumba.

It was nice of him to try to hold the crowd—and the *Best of* cameraman, who picked his camera up and began filming again—but it wouldn't last long. Soon, everyone would leave and they would have missed their chance.

Daisy stood beside Lula. "What rotten bad luck!" she said.

"Did this have to happen the night the *Best Of* people were filming?" Lula asked angrily.

"Miss, check please," one of Lula's customers requested. As she headed to the table, she noticed Enrique moving toward the stage. What was he doing?

She watched as he spoke quickly to Paulo and Ty. Paulo shook his head, but Enrique was persuading him of something. The next minute, Paulo returned to the microphone. "Let's hear it for Mr. Smedlinsky," he said.

The crowd applauded, but Mr. Smedlinsky kept dancing.

"Thank you, Mr. Smedlinsky," Paulo tried again.

Mr. Smedlinsky took no notice, swept away by his own dancing. "Thank you . . ."

Daisy shut off the boom box, jolting Mr. Smedlinsky from his private world of dance. He bowed to the audience and climbed down from the table.

"Good news," Paulo told the audience. "We're going to perform, after all."

The audience applauded enthusiastically as people who'd been getting up to leave sat back down. The *Best of* cameraman aimed his lens toward the stage.

Enrique picked up the *clave* sticks, holding them in the air and banging them together loudly. Lula realized it was the opening of her song, "Noche Loca."

Ty played his guitar, and Paulo began to sing the words. She was amazed by his voice. It was deep and strong. She never would have suspected he possessed the charismatic star power he radiated as he sang.

"Bang! Bang! Bang!
Going faster! Faster!
Soaring up through the summer night.
Bang! Bang! Bang!
Now the moon is throbbing!
Circled with sound.
Feeling so right."

Enrique handled the conga solo like a pro. It wasn't the same as when Paulo did it in rehearsal, but Lula thought it was even better. He played the congas with his whole gorgeous body, smashing the drums like a man possessed by some ancient demon. The front of his shirt became soaked with sweat, his face contorted in a kind of ecstacy.

The audience cheered and whistled. *"¡Wepa!"* a man shouted, and Lula saw that her father had come in with friends. Beth Minor from The "Best Of" Network was dancing in place while her camerman filmed.

Paulo sang the second verse that she'd added.

"Bang! Bang! Bang!
The conga in my chest beats!
My caliente heart heats.
Bang! Bang! Bang!
When I meet you in the night!
Congas play, the love pounds.
Feeling so right."

Ty began his sexy blend of rock and Spanish guitar. A rasping sound took her by surprise. Jeff was back! He came in from the kitchen wailing on the *güiro,* just as they'd rehearsed, and joined the others on the stage.

When he and Ty were done, the audience once again exploded with applause.

They repeated both verses again, and it was clear that CeCe had been right: The original song was just exactly what the band need in order to stand out. By the time they launched into the "La Vida Es un Carnaval" and "Livin' La Vida Loca" combination, Enrique had meshed smoothly with the others as if he'd been with them from the start.

He'd saved them, really—he'd made it possible for them to have their chance in the "Best Of" competition. If he hadn't jumped up there and taken charge, Noche Loca would have folded, just given up.

But if he'd let them fold, they would have been one less band to compete with.

Lula couldn't imagine why he'd done it.

Twenty

Lula's father and his friends were the last customers to leave at four in the morning, although the restaurant remained full until almost three. "Great song, Lulabelle," Ruben Cruz said, hugging Lula. "Maybe I don't deserve it, but you've made me a proud *papi.*"

"Thanks," she said, hugging him.

With a last good-bye to him, she locked the door and went over to the stage, where the guys were taking down the microphone and speakers. She looked at Enrique, not knowing what to say. Their eyes met, but Ty and Paulo were still there. It wasn't the time to talk.

She continued on into the kitchen, where Jeff, Marc, and Daisy were cleaning up. "It looks like a bomb blew up in here," she said with a laugh. Pots and dishes were piled in the sink, waiting to make it into the dishwasher. Food had spilled and was smeared everywhere.

Daisy tossed a sponge to her. "Join the party," she said.

Lula began wiping a counter. "How's CeCe?" she asked.

"I think she's got the flu or a virus of some kind," Marc answered. "She stayed to hear the band sing 'Noche Loca' and then went to her apartment."

"I just brought her some tea and toast," Daisy added. "She had it and went back to bed."

Daisy rinsed her sponge at the metal sink next to the dishwasher, where Jeff was stacking the next load of dishes. "You okay?" she asked quietly.

He waved his hand in a gesture that said *so-so*. "I don't feel wonderful about what happened," he admitted. "But it was my own fault for not being honest with her."

"Your great-grandmother came to the restaurant to see CeCe," Lula told him. "But CeCe doesn't know where they met before. Your great-grandmother looked familiar to her, though."

"I don't know how she wound up coming here," he said. "It almost seems like fate, doesn't it?"

"It must be a relief, in a way. Now you don't have to lie anymore," she said.

"Yeah—because she knows the truth, and also because I'll probably never see her again," Jeff said. "And she's probably angry at my grandmother and at my mother, too, for not telling her I'm gay. What a mess."

"Hmm," Lula agreed. "I'm glad you made it back for the set, though."

"Me too," Jeff agreed.

"And you can get CeCe some nice new countertops," she added. He looked at her quizzically. "Since you're a marble importer, and all."

Laughing, he threw a towel at her, which landed on her head and face. "Who turned out the lights?" Lula joked from under the cloth.

It took them nearly two more hours of

cleaning to get the kitchen back in order. Paulo and Ty stuck their heads in to say good night. Lula felt a pang of disappointment that Enrique had left without even saying good-bye.

She no longer knew if she was angry at him. Why did he have the lyrics to her song if he hadn't planned to steal them? What had Paco meant about his spying on the competition?

"I'd better go out front and sweep," Lula said, grabbing a broom and dustpan. She went into the restaurant and began sweeping. She quickly collected a good-size pile of dirt, but when she looked for the dustpan, it wasn't on the shelf where she'd left it.

"What are you waiting for?" Turning back toward the voice, she saw Enrique holding the dustpan to the floor for her to use.

She jumped back, startled, dropping the broom. "Where did you come from?"

"I was sitting in the corner, waiting for you," he explained. "You were so intent on your work that you didn't notice me, so I came to help. Can you spare a minute to talk?"

She nodded and sat down at a table. "The first thing I want you to see is this," he said. He went to the table where he'd been sitting and picked up a book. It was *Finding Fossils at the Midnight Laundromat.* "Open it to the page Nzoake autographed."

The book was autographed to her. "It's *my* copy," she said, not understanding. "Why do you have it?"

"Your copy must have gotten kicked under my couch the other day at my apartment," he said.

She smiled, remembering the time they'd had at his place. "Okay, I can imagine how that might have happened," she admitted.

He smiled back in a way that made her blush. "I don't have to imagine," he said, lowering his voice, "because I can remember, and it's all I've been thinking about."

She could feel herself melting toward him. In another second she'd be in his arms—and she wasn't ready for that. "If my book went under your couch, why do I have it upstairs?"

"You have *my* copy of the book. You must have picked it up by mistake after you left my apartment," he surmised. "You rushed out the door, if you remember. When you check, you'll see that the book you have upstairs is autographed to me."

Okay, that made sense, she supposed.

"But I heard what your friend Paco said," she insisted. "You were spying on me just so you could get some advantage in the competition."

"Paco is an idiot," Enrique said. "He's been telling me to get the lowdown on Noche Loca ever since he saw me with you one day at the beach. I never told my band anything except that Noche Loca wouldn't be easy to beat."

"Really?" Lula asked.

"Really," he said. Reaching into the pocket of his jeans, he pulled out a folded piece of paper. "I found this under the couch today. It must have fallen out of the book."

She took the paper from him and unfolded it. It was the poem she'd written about him, "Electric Storm." Now Lula was sure she was blushing. "I wrote this about you," she revealed.

"I was hoping," he said.

She leaned across the table, sliding her arms onto his shoulders. In seconds they were kissing—a long, deep kiss that Lula never wanted to end.

"Why aren't you getting ready for work?" Jeff asked Lula two weeks later.

"Not working," Lula replied brightly. She was sitting at their table counting cash, her tip money, to make a bank deposit. "CeCe hired three new servers, so I have a night off." That was fine with her. CeCe's Cuban Café had become so busy that she now made more money working four nights than she used to make when she worked six days, lunch and dinner shifts combined.

CeCe now happily shared the lead vocals with Paulo. Jeff ran back and forth from the stage to the kitchen. He was able to do this because CeCe had also hired more kitchen help to assist him.

"There are so many more people at CeCe's now," Lula commented. "It's so different."

"I know—people to bus the table, people to work the dishwasher, prep cooks, and a second full cook—it's almost like working in a real restaurant," Jeff said.

"It *is* a real restaurant. And you're running the kitchen," she said. "You're the head guy in charge."

"I suppose," he said halfheartedly.

She looked at him, concerned. It seemed to her that he hadn't completely gotten over coming out to Great-grandma Terrio in such a sudden and unexpected way. For someone who always assumed things would turn out well in the end, he'd been uncharacteristically down lately.

Marc only worked part-time in the kitchen these days, since he'd started working on a new show, an all-male production of *Romeo and Julio.*

Despite their busy schedules, Marc and Jeff spent a lot of time together. They seemed so well suited to each other.

It was the very fact that Jeff's life was going so well that worried Lula. His dream of running a kitchen in a South Beach hot spot had come true. He was in love with a great guy. Everything was great, and he should have been overjoyed. But what had happened between him and his great-grandmother was keeping him from just letting go and being happy about how great his life was.

There was a knock on the door. "It is me," CeCe shouted through the door. "I need you both."

Lula pulled open the door and was relieved to see that CeCe was smiling. "Come down to my apartment. They're airing *The Best of South Beach*. I've already told the others."

They hurried to CeCe's large, cheerful apartment, where the TV was on. Marc, Jon, Ethan, and Daisy were jammed onto the couch together. Paulo and Ty were perched on the couch's arms.

They already knew they hadn't won. The TV station had informed them within three days of the filming. Enrique and his band hadn't won either. The four "untouchable" groups Enrique had predicted would win were featured, plus another group they had never heard of. But, the "Best Of" people had put together a film montage of all the bands they'd liked. They'd assured CeCe that Noche Loca would appear in that.

Lula and Jeff brought in kitchen chairs and joined the others while CeCe busied herself putting out snacks.

They watched the program with casual interest, tickled to see places they knew, until the montage began. "There we are!" Jeff shouted. The group of them, as a whole, sat forward at once, riveted to the set.

The film was edited to show snippets of all the songs they'd sung. They'd even included a shot of CeCe talking to the audience before she'd gotten too sick to perform.

Suddenly, everyone cried out in surprise at once.

"That dodgy old codger!" Daisy shouted as they watched Mr. Smedlinsky dancing on the table. "He knew they'd film him!"

"He got more time than we did!" Ty observed, laughing.

"His business will be booming now," CeCe predicted as she set a tray of sodas down in front of them.

"Good! Then he'll be too busy to pester me," Daisy said. "He'll be fine as long as he keeps his clothes on."

"I don't know," Jon disagreed. "There's big money to be made on the nude beach."

Daisy shivered. "I don't want to think about Mr. Smedlinsky dancing on the nude beach. I've seen enough to last me a lifetime, thank you very much."

"You'll be seeing this clip of Mr. Smedlinsky all summer because The "Best Of" Network replays its shows a zillion times," Marc pointed out.

"But that means they'll also show Noche Loca a zillion times," Ethan commented. "And that's got to be good for business."

"*Muy bien,*" CeCe agreed. Lula thought that the woman's always ready smile had never been brighter than it was these last weeks. Singing again after so long seemed to fill her with joy, and she appeared to enjoy working with Paulo. They had begun rehearsing a few song duets where both of them shined. The newly brisk business had most likely lifted a lot of financial concerns from her shoulders as well.

The group thanked CeCe for her hospitality and got up to leave. Lula was the last at the door. Before she went out, CeCe tapped her on the shoulder. "Stay a minute, please," she requested.

Lula stepped back into the room. "What's up?"

"Three things," CeCe began. "I'd like to pay you for your song. I have asked my lawyer to write up a contract between us."

"You don't have to do that," Lula said.

"I want to. It is the right thing," CeCe insisted. "The second thing is this—have you written any more poems we can use as songs?"

"I have a silver notebook full of them," Lula told her. "I'll bring some to you and you can see what you think."

"I would love that," CeCe agreed. "A man from a record company gave me his card last night. But we need more original songs before we can go to him with a CD. Don't tell the others yet. I don't want to get their hopes up."

"That's so exciting," Lula said, smiling. "Can't I even tell Jeff?"

"I do not suppose you could keep a secret from him, even if you tried," CeCe said. "Okay, only Jeff. Speaking of Jeff, that is the third thing I wanted to speak to you about. He doesn't seem like himself lately. What is the problem?"

"I think it's what happened with his great-grandmother," Lula told her. "She seems like a mean old crab to me, but I guess she means a lot to him. He says he spent a lot of time with her when he was little and she's an important part of his life. Now he feels that he's disappointed her just by being who he truly is."

"That cannot be a good feeling," CeCe sympathized. "I know his great-grandmother from somewhere. Do you know where she lives?"

"She was staying at the Beach Paradise Hotel," Lula recalled. "Why?"

"I just wanted to know," CeCe said, writing the name of the hotel on a notepad. "What are you up to tonight?"

"Enrique and I are going for a sunset dinner cruise on a boat," Lula told her with a smile.

"You like that young man very much," CeCe observed.

"Very, very much," she agreed. "I can't believe someone like him is interested in me."

"You give him a lot," CeCe said. "You bring something more than a pretty face. You are full of spirit, and you open his eyes to new worlds of poetry and writing. Soon you will go to the university and you will have even more new learning to share."

Lula had almost forgotten about the University of Miami. She was spending every free moment with Enrique now. She couldn't imagine not seeing him every day. But she was scheduled to go in just a few weeks.

Twenty-one

Daisy pulled an armful of clothing on hangers from Lula's closet. "What do you want to do with all these big white shirts?" she asked. "I never see you wear them anymore."

Lula remembered when they were all she'd ever worn. "There's a giveaway box right there," she said, pointing. She went back to packing her underwear and sleepshirts into her suitcase.

Tonight her father would come with a van he'd borrowed from a friend to drive her and her things to the University of Miami dorm. Lately he'd been coming down to CeCe's often and she'd spent more time with him than ever before.

Her mother was arriving next week to help her register for classes. After that, she'd head back to Canada to film a TV pilot for a sitcom.

Jeff poked his head in. "Can I move into the bedroom yet?" he asked.

"Can't wait to get rid of me, I see," she joked.

"Can't wait to have a real bedroom," he admitted. "It's nothing personal."

"Well, it was nice of you to let me have it all this time," she said. "I'm going to miss you so much."

He put up two hands to ward off her sentiment. "Don't get mushy on me now. I'm only a half hour away. We'll see each other all the time."

"It won't be the same," she said sadly.

Jeff shook his head. "Oh, no. I'm not going through a big farewell scene since I'm going to see you again in two days. You'll get me to say all this nice stuff about you, like what a great friend you are and how I never would have had the guts to come down here on my own if wasn't for you and then—look out!—I'll just turn around and there you'll be, back as if you never left. No sir. Not me!" He was still talking as he headed for the door. "Uh-uh! I'm not falling for that one. Not me. . . ."

She could still hear him, even after he was out in the hall. "Think you can get me to say I'll miss you when all the while you're just planning to come back. No way. . . ."

Lula chuckled as she stared after him. "He's dealing with this in his own unique way, wouldn't you say?

When Daisy didn't answer, Lula turned and saw there were tears in her eyes. She crossed the room to hug her. "I'm really not going very far," she said.

"You might as well be in a rocketship headed for the moon," Daisy disagreed, wiping her eyes. "You'll meet all these smart successful university types and you'll forget all about us . . . about me."

"How could that happen?" Lula asked. "I never even had a real close girl pal until I met you. Daisy, I could never replace you. Who else is like you?"

"Nobody. It's true," Daisy admitted, sniffing. "I'm rather one of a kind. And we are true mates, aren't we?"

"Completely," Lula assured her.

They continued packing some of Lula's things, and discarding others, for another hour. Most of what she was bringing, she put in a trunk. The rest went in a suitcase.

Lula put her books and papers into a cardboard box. She put her silver notebook inside. She also packed her copy of *Doing the Shang-a-lang on Hip-Hop Street* and her signed copy of *Finding Fossils at the Midnight Laundromat.* Along with those she put the card she'd received from Nzoake Jones in which the poet had written:

> **What a song! What a night!**
> **The dazzling life spirit is in your**
> **words.**
> **Never stop creating.**
> **Your friend and fellow poet,**
> **Nzoake Jones**

"I'm famished!" Daisy announced. "Let's go down to the restaurant and get a bite."

"It's closed," Lula reminded her. "It's Monday, remember."

"CeCe's working down there with Marc and Jeff," Daisy said. "They're creating some new dinner special or some such thing. I'm sure we can coax a meal out of them."

They took the back stairs down. "Hello?" Lula called as they walked into the empty kitchen. She turned to Daisy. "No one's here."

"Maybe they're out front in the restaurant," Daisy suggested.

"I don't think so," Lula told Daisy, looking back over her shoulder as she pushed open the kitchen door toward the restaurant. "They're not—"

"SURPRISE!"

Lula's hands flew to her face in delighted amazement. "You guys!" she cried as she faced a room full of friends.

"We couldn't let you leave without a party!" Daisy said, laughing.

Ethan, Marc, and Jon had baked her a large sheet cake that was a beach scene with blue Jell-O for the water and white icing for sand. Gummy fish and other sea creatures swam in the gelatinous blue water while small naked dolls, male and female, stood on the icing. A small sign had the words NUDE BEACH written in icing. Also written in icing, it said: GOOD LUCK, LULA! REMEMBER US AND FUN IN THE SUN.

"It's a work of art!" Lula cried. "Thank you!"

Suddenly music filled the room. Mr. Smedlinsky came in at the head of a dance line of elderly women who had become his students as a result of seeing him on TV. From somewhere in the room, his boom box blasted a Latin beat. "Good luck! Lu-la!" the women and Mr. Smedlinsky sang in a staccatto beat as they danced around the room. "Good luck! Lu-la!"

"This is too awesome!" Lula cried, clapping her hands together.

"I told you there would be no big good-byes," Jeff teased, coming up alongside her.

She pushed him playfully. "I should have known."

Paulo and Ty waved to her and began playing on the stage. Ty's pretty, petite wife was there. She sat next to Paulo's tall, attractive, dark-haired wife—and their four children.

"I told you Paulo and Ty were gay," Jeff said, mocking himself for being so obviously mistaken.

"See what happens when you deal in stereotypes," she scolded with a smile. "Wow! What cute kids!"

Jeff hugged her. "If I thought you were going far, I'd be a basket case," he said, "but since—"

He broke off mid sentence, and Lula looked up to see what had distracted him.

CeCe had come in the front door. Great-grandma Terrio accompanied her.

Lula grabbed Jeff's hand. For a second he gripped her so tightly that her hand tingled. Then he let go. "Might as well go face the tiger," he said, sounding resolved.

"I'll go with you," she offered.

He nodded at her. "Thanks."

Together, hand in hand, they walked up to CeCe and Great-grandma Terrio.

"I remembered where I met your great-grandmother," CeCe spoke first. "It was nineteen fifty-five. I was singing in a gorgeous hotel in Havana, and Rose was a guest there. She came to hear me almost every night. We hit it off and even exchanged postcards for a while. But then I came to America and Rose moved to Italy and neither of us knew where the other was."

"When I read the article in the *Miami Herald,* I remembered CeCe's name," Great-grandma Terrio added. "I came to hear her wonderful voice again."

Lula was surprised the Great-grandma Terrio no longer seemed hostile to Jeff.

"That's wonderful, Great-grandma," Jeff spoke, his voice steady. "I'm sorry you had to find out the truth about me the way you did, but I'm glad you know. I love you and I want you to know who I am."

Tears brimmed in the old woman's eyes, and she held her arms open to him. He entered her embrace, squeezing tight. "I know who you are, my little Jeffy," she said to him.

"What happened?" Lula asked CeCe.

"I went to the hotel to talk to her," CeCe replied. "She's a good woman, just stuck in her old ways of thinking. I told her she's in America now—get with it!"

"You did?" Lula asked, surprised.

"I also reminded her that love and family are not things you should turn your back on so easily," CeCe added. "Before we left, she called Le Cordon Bleu College of Culinary Arts Miami."

"For Jeff?" Lula asked excitedly.

CeCe nodded. "If he wants to go, she will help him financially."

"That will rock his world," Lula said, beaming. "He'll flip."

She looked around the restaurant at all the new friends she'd made. Everything was just perfect—almost. "Isn't Enrique coming?" she asked CeCe.

"He's picking up something he ordered for you," she replied.

"What?" Lula asked.

CeCe winked mysteriously. "You'll like it."

In the next half hour he showed up, and Lula pulled him into a hug. She noticed that he had a small wrapped box in his hand. "What is it?" she asked.

"You'll see," he teased.

"Time for presents!" CeCe announced.

They gathered around a table, where Lula unwrapped a pile of gifts.

One very big box was from Daisy. It contained the trunk of pretty dresses and sandals from her friend who had run away with the biker. "She wrote and said to give them to someone who would like them,"

Daisy explained. "She only wears leather now, and you look better in the things than she ever did."

"An instant wardrobe. Thank you," Lula said.

Mr. Smedlinsky gave her a batch of gift coupons entitling her to free dance lessons. CeCe gave her a new notebook covered in fabric and beads. Jon and Ethan presented her with three videos of old Alfred Hitchcock movies that included *The Birds.* From Paulo she received a book on Florida restaurants, and Ty gave her a CD of Spanish guitar.

Together, Marc and Jeff presented her with a large black canvas bookbag with a photo of their smiling faces transferred onto the front. Jeff handed her one more neatly wrapped small box. "This one is just from me alone," he explained.

Lula opened it and began to laugh hard. She lifted the can of Funk-Off out of the box. "Everyone needs this!"

"It was time for a fresh can," Jeff explained.

She saved Enrique's gift for last. When she pulled the paper off, she uncovered an iPod. "This is too great!" she cried.

"Do you like it?" he asked.

She threw her arms around him. "It's perfect," she said. To her, it truly was the perfect gift, since music had played such an important part in their relationship.

Paulo and Ty began to play. Paulo's children joined in, playing the *claves*, the bell, the *güiro*, and a set of bongo drums.

Enrique took Lula by the hand and led her to a space that had been cleared for dancing. Although the music was fast, he locked his hands at the small of her back and swayed, holding her close.

"You'll see me on weekends, won't you?" she asked, resting her head on his shoulder.

"No," he replied.

She pulled back and stared at him, her brow knit in concern. "No?"

He smiled warmly back at her. "I'll see you more than that. I enrolled for two classes at the School of Music."

"You're kidding!" she cried. This was too good to be real.

"No kidding. I'll be there two days a week," he told her, "plus weekends. I didn't want to lose you to one of those college guys. And, anyway, if you go to college, I have to go to college. I can't let you outgrow me and leave me behind."

She gazed into those beautiful eyes with their gold and green flecks and thought that she saw—maybe for the first time—the real warm, generous person inside. He was still the hottest hottie in town, but now he was also something more to her: He was the one she loved.

She put her hand on his neck and kissed him hard on the lips—sure that she would never, ever, want to leave him behind.

Suzanne Weyn and Diana Gonzalez had the best time writing this book. Being on the lookout for comic situations, jokes, and wacky characters was lots of fun. When one suggested a joke, the other added to it, and then they collaborated and spun it all together. It made for a lot of laughs.

Diana Gonzalez loves animals and has worked as a veterinary assistant for the last four years while also attending school. She also teaches horseback riding and has a horse named Albert who she rides regularly. Diana especially enjoys studying art, creative writing, and Web design.

Suzanne Weyn enjoyed writing a funny romance, since her last novel for young adults, *The Bar Code Tattoo*, was a serious science-fiction thriller. It was a nice change. Suzanne says that though no one can make her laugh as hard as her sisters and brother—very funny people— she and Diana share a comic take on life that made writing this book together a natural fit.

LOL at this sneak peek of

She's Got the Beat
By Nancy Krulik

A New Romantic Comedy from Simon Pulse

"That country bumpkin is definitely not our kind," Erika agreed.

The words stung in Miranda's ears hours later as she sat alone in her room, staring at the peeling paint and feeling hideously alone. She was so embarrassed. Miranda wasn't usually the type to cause a scene—especially in a bar. But that guy Travis had crossed the line, and she'd instinctively lashed out. She'd tried calling Cally so she could cry on a friendly shoulder, but her best pal wasn't picking up her cell. As for her roommates, Missy was in her room with the door locked . . . again. And Kathleen was out. Probably staying at her boyfriend's place or something, Miranda figured.

There was nothing to do but study.

That was, after all, what she'd come to college for, wasn't it? To get an education. She hadn't come here to make friends or be popular. She would just bury herself in her work. That's all. The summer would go faster that way. Hell, maybe if she worked real hard she could get out of school in three years instead of four.

It wasn't a particularly comforting thought.

An hour or so later, Miranda's head was buried in her book when there was a knock at her door. "Yes?"

"It's Kathleen. I saw the light on in your room."

"Come on in," Miranda said, putting down her book and sitting up tall on her bed. "It's open."

"Studying on a Friday night?" Kathleen asked as she entered the room. "Girl, you need a life."

That's the understatement of the year. "I was out before, but . . ." No sooner were the words out of her mouth than the tears began to fall. Harsh, bitter tears, which seemed to burn the skin off her face. The story of the horrible night then poured out of her, every heinous detail—from start to finish. Kathleen listened to all of it, passing no judgment, until Miranda got to the part about decking Travis.

"All right, Miranda! The women of Texas should bow down and kiss your feet."

"That's not how Erika and Adrianna saw it," Miranda replied ruefully.

"Oh, and you're going to take the bimbo brigade seriously?" Kathleen asked.

"You know them?" Miranda asked, surprised.

"Well, maybe not those two personally, but I know their type. What were you doing with them, anyhow?"

Miranda shrugged. "They asked me to go to dinner. It didn't seem like it would be a bad idea. But I shouldn't have gone. I knew right away we weren't going to have a good time. I didn't fit in with them."

"You should be proud of that. You should also be proud of the fact that you stuck them with the check."

Miranda groaned. "Ooh, I forgot all about that. I'll give them the money on Monday."

"Why?" Kathleen asked. "Consider it an entertainment fee. After all, it sounds like you gave 'em quite a show."

Miranda blushed. "That's so not like me. I don't fight people. You should have known me back home. I'm really mellow. I just like to hang out with my crowd and . . . well, the thing is, I don't have any crowd here. I don't really fit in with anyone." She sighed.

"That's not so," Kathleen replied, sounding very indignant. "You fit in with *us*. For starters, I know Mother thinks the world of you."

Miranda frowned at the thought of the house mannequin, Mother. "Very funny."

"No, seriously. You and I aren't so different."

Miranda looked at Kathleen, with her dark black eyeliner, vintage Sex Pistols T-shirt, and varied piercings. What could she and this girl possibly have in common?

"We both came here knowing no one, trying to forge our own paths," Kathleen explained. "I picked one that's a whole hell of a lot different from who I was at home, and you probably will too. But you're never going to change until you break away from all those beliefs your parents and friends have crammed down your throat all these years."

"I'm not so sure I *want* to change."

Kathleen gave her a knowing look. "Okay, maybe not change, but *grow.* And you do want to do that. Otherwise, you would've stayed home and married that guy you told us about—what was his name? Donny?"

"Denny."

"Right. Denny. You would have married him and lived your little housewife life in your old hometown. But you came here. Obviously there was some part of you that didn't want to be stuck in a small-town rut. You came to Austin. That was your first step toward breaking free. Now you've got to try hard to completely break out of the mold. Do something a little crazy. Something completely out of character."

"I don't know what you mean."

Kathleen sighed. "There must be something you've always wanted to do or try that you just couldn't see yourself doing back in Boonton."

"Barton."

"Wherever," Kathleen said, and sighed. "The point is, you won't find out who you are unless you look for the one thing that makes you special, different. It's in there somewhere, buried under eighteen years of sweet, down-home conditioning."

"I guess . . . ," Miranda mused, sounding unsure.

"Well, at least think about it, okay?"

Miranda nodded.

"And in the meantime, why don't you and I go down to the kitchen? I think I spotted a whole container of Chunky Monkey in the freezer."

"Okay," Miranda agreed. "And while we're at it, we can go really crazy and pour chocolate sauce all over it."

Kathleen chuckled. "Now you're getting in the spirit."

☆

The house was really quiet when Miranda awoke on Saturday morning. Rather than sit around by herself—again—she decided to get moving and explore the ultracool neighborhood she'd seen the first day she'd arrived.

As she hopped off the bus in the West End, Miranda spotted a local Starbucks and quickly ran in for a large Frappuccino to go.

Mmm . . . a sip from home. That was the nice thing about chains like Starbucks, Burger King, and the Gap. They all looked the same, no matter which one you went to. They were like familiar neighbors that traveled with you wherever you went.

Of course, familiarity, and same-old—same-old were the exact root of her troubles, at least according to Kathleen. Miranda guessed she probably should have at least stopped in the little café on the corner for an ice coffee. At least it would have been a little bit different.

She glanced at the store window in front of her. The clothes were definitely not her usual style. The mannequins were all clothed in tight, brightly colored skirts, belly shirts, and jeweled high-heel shoes. For a moment Miranda considered going inside and trying something on, but then she thought better of it. Those clothes would look a whole lot better on Mother than they ever would on her.

And then something caught her eye that struck her as a perfect fit. A little sign, stapled to a post on the sidewalk, it read:

DISCOVER THE BEAT OF YOUR OWN DRUMMER.
Learn to drum from one of Austin's top percussion teachers. All levels welcome.

Then it listed a phone number and an address. Miranda didn't know why the sign had gotten her attention; it was just a small, plain sheet of paper. But now that she'd focused on it, she couldn't seem to turn away. *Drum lessons.* That sounded kind of cool. Very un-Miranda. Which was exactly what the doctor—or, in this case, *Kathleen*—had ordered.

Of course, she'd never thought of herself as particularly musical—or rhythmical. She chuckled to herself, remembering the time her daddy had tried to teach her the Texas two-step before a father-daughter dance at the middle school. She just couldn't stick with the beat, and wound up stepping on her dad's feet more than the floor. *Drumming— yeah, right. What was she thinking?*

Still, she checked the map she'd been carrying in her purse, and tried to locate the address. Hmm . . . it wasn't far, just a block or two. She could find it easily. The fact that the drum studio was so close and easily accessible struck Miranda as some sort of sign. She turned and headed off toward the studio. It couldn't hurt to just get some information, anyway.

The address on the sheet led Miranda to a small music shop on a nearby side street. It seemed small for a place where they gave drum lessons. At least from what Miranda could tell, the store was filled with music books and instruments for sale. She walked up to the counter and approached a heavy-set man with a shaved head. He was wearing a short-sleeve shirt and khaki shorts. He had a large tattoo on his forearm, and wore several thick silver rings, one of which looked like a skeleton's head. "Excuse me," she said shyly. "I, um . . . came to ask you about the drum lessons. I saw the sign on a pole on Sixth Street and—"

The balding guy nodded. "Oh, you want *Paul*," he said. He turned toward a stairwell just behind the counter. "Paul," he shouted downstairs, "some girl's here about your ad."

Miranda breathed a sigh of relief. So this fellow wasn't the drum teacher after all. Well, that was a good thing. She couldn't see herself spending any time alone in a studio with someone so menacing.

But she could see herself spending time with him. . . . , Miranda's eyes burst open wide, and her heart pounded slightly as quite possibly the most gorgeous specimen of masculinity she'd ever seen emerged from the stairwell. He looked about twenty or twenty-one, and he was tall and muscular, with large green eyes and blondish short hair. His face was perfectly oval shaped, and he had just the hint of a cleft in his chin.

"Hi. I'm Paul."

Miranda blushed, realizing suddenly that she had been staring—no, make that *gaping*—at the man in a pretty obvious fashion. She stuck out her hand quickly. "I'm Miranda. I . . . um . . . well . . . I saw your sign on the post, and drumming sounded cool, even though I'm not really very musical, and . . ." *Ah, jeez. Could she sound any more stupid?*

But Paul didn't seem to think she sounded idiotic. In fact, he smiled again. "It *is* pretty cool. And I'll bet you're more musical than you think. Most people are."

Miranda shrugged. "I don't know about that."

"Only one way to find out," Paul replied, pointing his hand in the direction of the stairwell. "I have a small kit set up downstairs. Why not give it a try now?"

Now? "Well, I . . . I mean . . .the thing is . . ." *There she went again, sounding like a complete idiot.*

"Come on," Paul urged.

The idea of going downstairs with this guy definitely didn't sound too unpleasant. But there *was* one problem. "I don't have a lot of money with me," Miranda told him.

"That's okay," he assured her. "The first lesson's a free trial."

"It is?" said the big guy behind the counter, sounding surprised. "Since when?"

"Since this charming person walked into the shop, Jerry," Paul told him. "Come on, Miranda. What have you got to lose?"

Perfect Strangers

Mixed Messages

The Write Stuff

Coming Soon: Message in a Bottle

LOVE
LETTERS

Jahnna N. Malcolm

A deliciously romantic series
about sweeties, crushes,
and the hottie next door

**In Love Letters,
you have to read
between**

the

lines.

Published by Simon Pulse

NEWLY WED

Nancy Krulik

The honeymoon just ended.
And Jesse and Jen are about to
get a hilarious helping of reality.

It's a year in the life of one young couple, two
opinionated best friends, and more meddling
family members than you can count.

This I swear.

PUBLISHED BY SIMON PULSE